a friend at midnight

ALSO BY CAROLINE B. COONEY

The Janie Books
The Face on the Milk Carton
Whatever Happened to Janie?
The Voice on the Radio
What Janie Found

The Time Travel Quartet
Both Sides of Time
Out of Time
Prisoner of Time
For All Time

Other Books
Diamonds in the Shadow
Hit the Road
Code Orange
The Girl Who Invented Romance
Family Reunion
Goddess of Yesterday
The Ransom of Mercy Carter
Tune In Anytime
Burning Up
What Child Is This?
Driver's Ed
Twenty Pageants Later
Among Friends

a friend
at midnight

CAROLINE B.
COONEY

WATERBROOK
PRESS

A Friend at Midnight
Published by WaterBrook Press
12265 Oracle Boulevard, Suite 200
Colorado Springs, Colorado 80921
A division of Random House Inc.

ISBN 978-1-4000-7209-5

Published in the United States by WaterBrook Multnomah, an imprint of The Doubleday Publishing Group, a division of Random House Inc., New York.

WaterBrook and its deer colophon are registered trademarks of Random House Inc.

This book is copublished with Delacorte Press an imprint of Random House Children's Books, a division of Random House Inc.

The Library of Congress cataloged the hardcover edition as follows:
Cooney, Caroline B.
A friend at midnight / Caroline B. Cooney. — 1st ed.
p. cm.
Summary: After rescuing her younger brother abandoned at a busy airport by their divorced father, fifteen-year-old Lily finds her faith in God sorely tested as she struggles to rescue herself from the bitterness and anger she feels.
[1. Brothers and sisters—Fiction. 2. Family problems—Fiction. 3. Christian life—Fiction.]
I. Title.

PZ7.C7834Fr 2006
[Fic]—dc22   2006004598

Printed in the United States of America
2008—First WaterBrook Press Trade Paperback Edition

10 9 8 7 6 5 4 3 2 1

a friend at midnight

part one:
september

chapter 1

For miles, nobody spoke.

Then the driver stopped right in the road and said, "Get out of the car."

Michael's fingers struggled with the latch of his seat belt. The driver reached over with such irritation Michael expected a slap, but the driver just released Michael's seat belt. It was gray and shiny and slid away like a snake.

The car door was heavy. Michael opened it with difficulty and climbed out onto the pavement. The passenger drop-off made a long dark curve under the overhang of the immense airport terminal. Glass doors stretched as far as Michael could see. Men and women pulled suitcases on wheels and struggled with swollen duffel bags. They hefted briefcases and slung the padded straps of laptop carriers over their shoulders. The glass doors opened automatically for them and the airport swallowed them.

"Shut the door, Michael," said the driver.

Michael stared into the car. He could not think very clearly. The person behind the wheel seemed to melt and re-form. "You're not coming?" Michael whispered.

The driver answered, and Michael heard the answer. But he knew right away that he must not think about it. The shape and contour of those syllables were a map of some terrible unknown country. A place he didn't want to go.

"Shut the door," repeated the driver.

But Michael could neither move nor speak.

Again the driver leaned forcefully over the passenger seat where Michael had sat. Michael backed up, the heels of his sneakers hitting the curb. The driver yanked the door shut and the car began leaving before the driver had fully straightened up behind the wheel.

Michael stared at the back of the car, at its trunk and license plate, and immediately his view was blocked by a huge tour bus with a red and gold logo. Passengers poured out of the bus, encircling Michael, talking loudly in a language he did not know.

The bus driver opened low folding doors covering the cargo hatch and flung luggage onto the sidewalk. Bus passengers swarmed around the suitcases. Michael watched as if it were television. When all the luggage had been distributed, the driver folded the doors back, leaped into his bus and drove off.

Michael could see down the road again, but the car that had dropped him off was long gone. AIRPORT EXIT, said the sign above the road.

Three cars drove up next to his feet. Families got out.

People kissed good-bye. They vanished into the maw of the airport. Another bus arrived, all its passengers either old ladies carrying big purses or old men carrying canes and newspapers.

Michael felt eyes on him. Not bus people eyes, because the bus people were too busy making little cries of pleasure as they spotted their suitcases.

He didn't have to look to know they were police eyes focused on him. He was not going to tell the police. Not now, not ever.

Michael eased into a knot of bus people, resting his hand on the edge of an immense suitcase towed by a fat chatty lady. Another even fatter lady towed an even larger suitcase. Wherever they were going, they could hardly wait to get there. The ladies hauled their suitcases into the terminal. Michael went with them. The women never noticed him, but surged forward into a ladies' room. Michael stood in the midst of a vast open area. Hundreds of passengers hurried by, separating on either side of him as if he were a rock in a river. They gave him no more attention than they would have given to such a rock.

Michael threaded his way down the concourse until he came to flight monitors high on the wall. Michael was not a good reader. Charts, like the departure and arrival lists on these screens, were difficult for him. Craning his neck and squinting, he struggled to interpret the information. There were several flights to LaGuardia. He counted six in the next two hours. He hung on to this information, as if it might be useful.

Michael was wearing new jeans. It was too hot for jeans, but he had been told to put them on. The crisp pant legs were rough against his skin. His T-shirt, though, was old and soft. It had been his sister Lily's, and he had filched it from her to use as packing around a fragile possession. He had been wearing it lately, even though it came to his knees.

He felt those eyes again. He walked into the men's room to get away from the stare. It was packed. So many men. Fathers, probably, or grandfathers or stepfathers or god-fathers. He closed himself in a stall, but the toilet was flushing by itself, over and over, as if it intended to drown him, and he fled from the wet sick smell of the place.

Back in the open space, Michael distracted himself by looking everywhere, even up. The ceilings were very high, with exposed girders in endless triangles that looked like art. He had been in this airport once before and had imagined swinging from those girders, leaping from one to the next, sure of his footing. Michael was not sure of anything right now, not even the bottoms of his feet.

He sat on a black bench that had curled edges, like a licorice stick. Ticket counters stretched in both directions: American, Southwest, Continental, Frontier, Delta. People stood in long slow lines that zigzagged back and forth, separated by blue sashes strung between chrome stands.

Maybe I just didn't understand, he thought. Maybe the car just went to park. Maybe if I go back outside . . .

He felt better. He went back outside.

Taxis and hotel limousines and vans from distant parking lots were driving up. Wheeled suitcases bumped over the tiled sidewalk as loudly as guns shooting. Clumps of people stumbled against him and moved on. New buses took the place of the last set, and their exhausts were black and clotted in his lungs.

The terrible words the driver had flung at Michael had been lying on that sidewalk, waiting for him to come back, and now the words jumped up and began yelling at him.

Michael tripped over a suitcase and fell hard on the

pavement. The suitcase owner picked Michael up, dusted him off and examined his bare elbows for scratches. "I'm sorry about that," said the man pleasantly. "You okay?"

Michael could hardly hear the speech of the man, banging against those terrible last words from the car. He couldn't answer.

"Where's your mom and dad, kiddo? Who are you with?" asked the man.

Michael recovered. "My grandmother," he said, astonished by how easily the lie came to him. Michael was not much of a fibber. He had always meant to get good at lying, because he was always leaving tracks he'd like to cover, but he never got around to thinking of good lies, and stupid ones were too stupid to bother with, so usually he just admitted whatever he'd done.

Where had that fib come from? Had the bottom of his mind been getting ready to lie?

"Where is your grandmother?" asked the guy, standing tall and scouting out the sidewalks.

"In the bathroom," said Michael. "She has to go a lot. I figured I had time to look around."

The guy laughed. "Better find her before she panics."

"Okay," said Michael. "Thanks." He went into the terminal again and did not look back.

This time when he walked past the ticket counters, he saw that they broke in the middle and that beyond them was another huge hallway. Michael entered new territory and slid gratefully into a magazine shop.

There were clerks at three registers and a line at each one. Every passenger at the entire airport was buying a snack before boarding. Michael had not had supper last night, and of course this morning there had been no breakfast, and now it was almost lunchtime. He walked around, staring at the racks of small bags. Honey mustard pretzels and jelly beans. Peanut butter cups and barbecue-flavored potato chips. Sugar-free gum and chocolate bars.

Usually Michael didn't care that much about food. His big sisters, now, Reb and Lily, they loved food. They were always moaning how they couldn't have this or shouldn't have that, because they might gain a pound. Looking at this food, Michael got hungry. But if he stayed, pretty soon the clerks would notice him.

Michael went back into the hallway. The next store sold gifts. Its front display held teddy bears. He studied the one in front, bright red and not half as good a bear as York.

Michael had gotten York when he was very small. York was very soft and easily squished, rusty brown the way a bear should be, with a knitted New York Yankees sweater and a tiny New York Yankees baseball cap. York had not washed well. One arm—Michael considered it York's pitching arm—had come off and although Michael carefully kept the arm for months, eventually it got lost. York's fur had acquired lavender streaks, something his mother blamed on bleach.

For years now, Michael had been trying not to sleep with York. He had graduated to keeping York in a cardboard box under the bed. That way, when Michael's friends came over to play, York was hidden. But at night, when he was tucked in, and the lights were off, Michael's hand would sneak out from under the covers and wave into the darkness under the bed until his fingers located the cardboard. Slowly, carefully, he would pull the box out into the room and go to sleep holding on to York's remaining arm.

York had seemed perfectly safe under the new bed. But he hadn't been.

Michael thought about his possessions, still sitting in the

new room. What would happen in that new room now? When he was ordered into the car, Michael had not known what the plan was. He hadn't known they were going to the airport. He had brought nothing with him.

Nothing.

He had not known the meaning of that word before. He had nothing.

He walked past more stores.

His sisters loved shopping even more than food. How many hours had Michael spent with his feet dangling from some bench while his sisters fingered every single sweater in a store the size of a stadium? And when his sisters were finally done shopping, what did they have to show for it? Usually nothing. They never had any money, either.

Michael wanted his sisters so much that for a terrible moment he thought he might cry.

He paused at a restaurant with two hostesses. They weren't busy—the restaurant was almost empty. The women frowned slightly, watching this eight-year-old all by himself. It had been a mistake to stop walking because one hostess opened her mouth to speak. Michael averted his face and yelled down the hall, "Mom! Wait up!" He broke into a run and ran smack into the security gates.

Passengers were hefting bags onto the X-ray conveyor belt and tossing their car keys and shoes and change into little boxes. On the far side, they were being wanded by security people or putting their shoes back on. There were three types of security: people in uniforms like flight attendants wore; people in police uniforms; and people in camo, probably National Guard.

It was a policewoman who spotted him.

He didn't move fast enough. The officer was next to him, bending over, smiling, and he couldn't let her ask questions, because he didn't have answers, so he smiled back and said, "I can't find the bathroom. My mom let me go to the bathroom and now I can't find it."

She led him back the way he'd come, to a different break between the ticket counters; another route to the front half of the terminal. "There it is," she said, pointing.

"Thanks!" Michael trotted, as if he were desperate, and he was desperate, just not for a bathroom. He killed time in there, seeing which soap spout actually delivered soap, and this time when he went back toward the shops, he found a little-kid playroom behind a stairwell. He joined children playing on toy trucks that doubled as benches for the parents.

On a far wall were pay phones. The phones had no booths and no seats. Not one was in use. Probably most people had cell phones. Michael did not have a cell phone. Mom and Kells and Reb and Lily all had cell phones but Michael was "too young." He had said a hundred times to his mother that nobody was "too young" for a phone.

I could call home, thought Michael.

But if Mom or Kells answered, Michael would have to hang up, because he wasn't ever telling the thing that had happened and the thing that had been said, and since he knew already he would just hang up on them, what was the point of calling?

Unless he could be sure of reaching Lily.

Somehow, Lily had known he would need to call home. She had been so sure, she'd trained him. What exactly had Lily known that Michael had not known?

Lily was fifteen and difficult. Michael adored her but steered clear if he could manage it. The day before he left, when he was literally hopping with joy, Lily dragged him into her bedroom and slammed the door. "It won't work,

Michael," she said, referring to his Plan. "But since you're going anyway, you're going to memorize something."

How Michael was looking forward to a life with no big sisters pushing him around. "No," he told Lily.

"Yes. Or I'll stomp you." Lily stomped him routinely and then said innocently to their mother, "Me? Fighting?"

Oh, well, he had told himself. Tomorrow Lily will be history. "Fine," he said grumpily to the sister he was sick of. "What do I have to memorize?"

Now in the airport, Michael picked up the phone. His throat was sore. He closed his eyes and saw the memorized number, all those digits. He dialed the phone company's 800 number and then he dialed his own area code and phone number. The phone pinged and told him to dial the number being billed. You always had to think about money, Lily had explained.

Again Michael poked the numbers for his home phone and this time he added Mom's PIN number. For years, her PIN number had been 3000, because she said that three children in the house felt like three thousand, especially when the three children were Rebecca and Lily and Michael. But then Mom got remarried, and a year later, Nathaniel was born. Mom went and got a new PIN number: 4000.

Lily said Mom had no right to get divorced, no right to get remarried, no right to have another kid, and absolutely no right to go and change her PIN number.

Michael, however, thought 4000 was an excellent PIN number because Nathaniel had four thousand toys and had broken four thousand pieces off things (mostly Michael's things) and had definitely worked through four thousand diapers. Every night felt like four thousand nights, too, because Nathaniel could not fall asleep without sobbing for half an hour.

They were all pretty grumpy about Nathaniel. Especially Michael, because he had to share a bedroom with this unwanted half brother. Kells built a double-sided bookcase across the bedroom, which supposedly gave Michael privacy but really just turned Nathaniel's side into an echo chamber. At least Nathaniel was still in a crib. He was old enough to climb out but never had and Michael certainly never demonstrated. Nathaniel belonged in a cage.

When Michael left home, Nathaniel had been twenty-two months old and Michael had figured not to see him again for a year. But his brother would still be twenty-two months old when Michael got back.

The call went through. Michael pictured all the phones and all their ringing: the kitchen phone in the great messy sunny room where everybody was always cooking; the portable phone in Mom and Kells's room; the TV room phone.

He hung up in the middle of the second ring.

It was too early to call.

Things might change.

* * *

Lily was putting Nathaniel down for his nap. When the phone rang, she was delighted, because Nate, like some little trained dog, honored the ring of a phone. Reb and Lily often called each other on their cell phones just to shut Nate up for a minute.

"I'll be right back, Nate," Lily told him. "I have to answer the phone. You put your head down and close your eyes. Before you know it, my phone call will be over and I'll be back."

Nate was still pretty easy to dupe. He said, "Okie, Wiwwy," which was how he said "Okay, Lily," and even though Lily tried to harden her heart against Nate, she adored him when he put his head down and murmured, "Okie, Wiwwy."

Lily whipped out of the room without looking into Michael's half. Michael's three quarters, actually. Nate had exactly enough space for his crib and one person to stand next to it.

Michael had stripped his side of every possession, taking every baseball card and toy truck and Lego and book and video game and CD and of course York. He had even taken the sheets off his bed—Michael!—who believed that laundry belonged on the floor and changing sheets was for sissies. After Michael threw his used sheets in the laundry room that day, he came back to admire the bare mattress: Proof. He was leaving. For good.

Lily understood Michael's decision to go. They all wanted to storm away when Mom remarried and they all wanted to storm away again when Nathaniel was born. But when Michael really did storm away, Lily knew in her heart why she and Reb had not. They knew better.

It gave Lily a bit of peace to know that Michael had York the Bear with him. York would never let Michael down.

The second ring was cut short. There was not a third one. Lily pounded down the stairs to look at the caller ID on the kitchen phone and see who had hung up. Probably some solicitor who had managed to avoid the Do Not Call list.

Lily adored the telephone. She loved e-mail and text messaging, because she loved every variation on communicating, but mostly Lily loved the sound of her own voice. Just since yesterday's phone calls, she had a hundred new things to tell every friend she had. If she got lucky,

Nathaniel would fall asleep and give her two fine nap hours for phone calls.

Mom and Kells would not be back till after midnight. They had driven Reb to college. It was the first semester of Reb's freshman year, and Lily had been counting the days right along with her sister, excited about seeing the campus and the dorm, meeting the roommates, helping unpack, hanging clothes and posters. But when the last box and suitcase had been wedged into the car, there was no room for Nate's car seat and no room for Lily.

"That works!" cried her sister brightly. "You guys stay here."

Lily was crushed. "Let's divide everything in two cars," she offered quickly. "Mom drives one car, Kells drives one. No fair leaving me and Nate behind."

How pleadingly her older sister looked at her. Reb, like Michael, wanted to enter a new world. She didn't even intend to use her nickname from now on. Michael had left forever, and now Reb would turn into some college woman named Rebecca, while Lily would be abandoned in a swamp of dirty diapers and educational toys.

Their house was chaotic in the best of circumstances, because not only did Mom drop everything everywhere, using the dining room table to match socks and the living room rug for stacking catalogs, but she piled her concert band's music on the stairs and left broken school instruments she needed to repair on the kitchen counter and lost whole series of CDs under the sofa. Lily even saw a cell phone peeking out from under a sloppy heap of paper napkins. Had to be Mom's—everybody else held tightly to essentials, or they would vanish forever in Mom's chaos. It was hard to believe that their messy mother easily controlled a four-hundred-student band program. Today the house was strewn with stuff Reb wasn't taking after all. Styrofoam packing peanuts lay like snow, and under all this was the debris of a toddler.

Lily had only one gift for a sister who wanted out. She managed a smooth smile for Reb and Mom. "Nate and I will be fine on our own. You guys drive safely."

Mom was anxious. "It's such a long time, though. It's a six-hour drive, more if there's traffic. We can't be back till after midnight. What if something happens?"

"Then I'll handle it," said Lily. She decided not to tell Mom about the cell phone under the paper napkins. A phone in her purse would mean Mom calling twenty-five times to check up on Lily. What could possibly happen that Lily couldn't handle?

Yet the sight of her family driving away had been awful, as if they were being sucked down a tube, never to return. Then of course Nathaniel wanted to play Jump Off the Back Step, a game that involved jumping off the back step. Lily's job was to applaud and cry, "Wow!" with lots of emphasis on the *w*, and Nate would whisper "Wow"—a good word for him, since he had *w* nailed. They played Jump Off the Back Step until Lily figured that even losing Reb and Michael wasn't as bad as playing Jump Off the Back Step one more time, so she coaxed Nate in for a very early lunch of tuna salad. Nate loved tuna salad. He always had cat breath because he did not love having his teeth brushed.

Now he was down for his afternoon nap way too early because she was the one ready for a nap.

Lily reached the kitchen. The stingy tart smell of the Magic Marker with which Reb labeled her boxes mixed with the fishy scent of tuna salad she'd forgotten to refrigerate. On the kitchen phone, the caller ID showed some out-of-state number. Undoubtedly a sales call. Kells was polite to telephone salespeople. "I'm so sorry," he would say, "we don't purchase items over the phone, but thank you anyway." Mom handled it differently.

"Stop phoning me!" she would shout. "I'm never going to want it, whatever it is! Hang up! You hang up first, do you hear me?"

Neither approach worked. Neither, apparently, did signing up for Do Not Call.

Lily deleted the number.

* * *

Michael continued to hold the receiver. Even though he was connected to nothing, he felt safer hanging on.

A shadow fell across him. He looked up to see a uniformed officer standing over him. Michael was not allowed to watch shows like COPS because of the violence, but of course he watched them all the time anyway, and he knew what police did in situations like this. They went after the dad.

"Hi," said Michael. "Is that a real gun?" Michael knew perfectly well it was a real gun. This was a cop. What would he have—a cardboard gun? "Have you ever used it?" said Michael. "My mom doesn't like guns. She won't let one in the house."

The officer smiled. "It is real and your mom is making a good decision."

Michael turned to the phone, hoping the officer would leave.

No such luck. "Where are your folks?" said the cop. His voice was pleasant and warm.

Michael gestured vaguely. "I just called my sister," he

said. "She's leaving for college." He was seized by horror. When was Reb leaving? What if they had already left? All of them? What if his house was empty? What if he called and the phone rang and rang and rang and rang—*and nobody came*? What was he going to do?

"Well, it was nice to talk to you," he said to the cop, letting go of the comforting phone. It was like letting go of York in the dark. "Bye." He was only steps from the parents on toy wagons. He needed parents so the cop would forget about him. But all the parents were paying close attention to their children and would speak up if he tried to look like theirs.

There was one couple kissing and smooching over by the windows. They looked as if they had no children; as if they never planned to have children. Michael flopped down at their feet, flat on his face, and hoped for the best. He felt sick from not eating and his head whirled. Under the seats lay used coffee cups and discarded magazines. He could see the feet of the officer, who was moving on, satisfied.

How silent the house was.

Lily put the tuna salad into the refrigerator.

It was quiet times that bothered her most these days. Michael had been a nonquiet brother.

Michael was a very busy kid, and most of all, he was busy talking: he talked all the time to everybody. He was busy with sports: hitting balls, kicking balls, pitching balls, dunking balls. He was busy going places: on foot, on bike, on skateboard. He was busy with projects and friends, busy in the cellar, busy in the attic, busy in the yard.

He was a dirty noisy nosy little eight-year-old.

One thing that kept him busy was making lists of everything he planned to do next. "I want to learn how to fish," he would say. "I want to scuba dive." He loved equipment. You could never have enough equipment.

Lily remembered Michael sitting by the road with all his equipment, waiting. Silent, because in all those hours, nobody—including Michael—knew what to say.

And then once Michael was gone, Nathaniel too got quieter, now that he didn't have to drown out his big brother. Lily almost wanted to wake Nathaniel up just to have company. Then she came to her senses and turned on the television.

She was setting down the remote when her thumb slid across the number pad, and other numbers filtered through her mind and she recognized the area code of that phone number on the caller ID.

She clicked off the television. A little prickle of fear entered her heart.

She had deleted the number from the kitchen phone but Mom's bedroom phone had a memory bank. Lily never went in there because she didn't like thinking about Mom and Kells sharing a room. She went upstairs on tiptoe so Nathaniel wouldn't sense her presence. She crept into the master bedroom and lifted the portable phone from its cradle to take back downstairs.

She peeked in on Nate. He was asleep in the flung-out way of toddlers—arms and legs all over the place.

Michael followed a small girl into a big yellow and blue play plane. Inside were little seats. He squashed himself beneath one. I could hide here for a long time, he thought. And then what?

He decided to check the sidewalk one more time.

Just in case.

He didn't see any of the people who'd shown interest in him before. He passed the ticket counters safely and walked out next to a janitor pushing a cleanup cart. Outside, he pressed against a cement pillar to avoid being mowed down by crossing guards and airplane crews, by suitcases and dogs in cages, sidewalk check-in staff and overflowing luggage trolleys.

A long thin blue bus arrived. AIRPORT PARKING, said the sign in its front window.

A woman next to Michael on the sidewalk called anxiously to the driver, "Do you stop at Parking Lot A?"

"We stop at all of 'em, lady. A, B, C, D, whatever letter you want."

The school buses at his new school had been named for letters. Michael had gotten on the wrong bus. It had not been his first failure, just one in a string. Michael went back inside so he didn't have to think about A, B, C, D and failure. When he found himself in the playroom again, near the wall phones, the one he had used before was ringing.

Lily let the phone ring. On the seventh ring, she thought, What kind of loser can't get to a phone in seven rings or else have their answering machine pick up?

"Wiwwy," called Nathaniel. He'd slept fifteen minutes instead of two hours. It was her own fault for putting him down early. He was capable of yelling "Wiwwy" several hundred times before tiring of the syllables.

"I'm on the phone, Nathaniel!" she yelled, and while she was yelling, somebody picked up at the other end. They didn't say anything. They just breathed. Lily got irritated. She was pretty nearly always irritated at how other people conducted their lives. "Who is this?" she demanded.

There was a long jagged intake of air at the other end and then sobs spurted out of the phone. Raw sobs, like cuts, like opening a can and slicing your palm with the lid.

I knew, thought Lily. I knew from the area code.

Except her brother Michael didn't ever cry. He didn't cry when a baseball hit him in the face. He didn't cry when he fell off his bike and ripped open his knees. He didn't cry when he got shots. He didn't cry when their parents' marriage ended and he didn't cry when their mother went into a new one. Michael didn't cry.

"Michael?" said Lily.

"Yes."

"Tell me what's happening. Where are you? What phone number is this? Why didn't you let it ring when you called a minute ago? What's wrong?"

There was another sob, drier this time; shallower.

From his crib, Nathaniel heard her say "Michael?" and since Nate loved Michael, he stopped shouting "Wiwwy" and started shouting "Miikooooo!"

Lily said, "Mom and Kells took Reb to college, Michael, and there wasn't enough room in the car for Nate and me, so we're here by ourselves. There's nobody around to butt in, Michael. Tell me what's happening."

"Lily," he whispered.

Lily waited. But Michael had nothing else to say. "I love you," Lily told him. She never said things like that. Even when he'd left forever, she had not told Michael she loved him.

She could hear the little huffs of his breathing, his effort to still the sobs.

Her heart was crumpled newspaper and kindling. Fear for her brother was the match. Flame charred a corner of Lily's heart.

"I'm here," she said.

When he'd left, Michael had done his own packing.

Mom had been beside herself about the whole thing because Michael's choice was a personal defeat, an assault. She seemed to think if she didn't pitch in, it wouldn't happen.

Michael didn't care. When Mom wouldn't help, he hiked a mile to the nearest strip of stores, collected cardboard boxes and carried them home, stacked inside each other. He did this five times. He filled them with his belongings and sealed them with strapping tape. He wrote his name and the precious new address in large fat black letters on all four sides, with big arrows pointing up.

On the day Dad was to arrive and take him away for good, Michael was up before dawn. Actually, Lily was pretty sure he'd never gone to bed. By the time the sun was up, Michael had dragged everything he owned to the road. Not the porch, not the back door, not the driveway— but the road. He was disowning the rest of them. He propped his fishing poles and baseball bat and bike against the boxes.

He had forgotten to pack clothing. Nothing that sat in a bureau drawer or hung on a hanger mattered to Michael. Mom gave up and dragged out two large suitcases. She folded every shirt carefully. Paired the socks. Replaced a broken lace on a sneaker.

Silently, the family moved through the house, finding things Michael had forgotten. Reb brought his baseball glove.

Mom brought his toothbrush, toothpaste and orthodontic appliance, which he had never worn and never would, but he let her drop the stuff into his duffel along with a book (as if Michael planned to do any reading again in this life) and an apple for a snack (as if he planned to choose apples once Mom wasn't supervising).

York lay in his usual box. The box wasn't marked because Michael could not possibly confuse York's box with ordinary boxes. Lily had a bad feeling about letting their father see York. She got her own backpack and silently transferred both York and box into that. It was the closest she came to telling Michael she loved him. When she slipped her backpack onto her brother's thin little shoulders and adjusted the straps, Michael hugged her, and this was new for both of them and they ended it quickly.

And then the hours passed.

Dad did not come. He did not call to say where he was, or when he was coming. Or if.

Mom brought Michael a bagel with cream cheese, but Michael shook his head, eyes fixed on the road.

The morning ended. Michael did not move. Michael who was nothing but movement—an eight-year-old whirlwind.

Neighbors phoned, asking for updates. Mom tried to be glad she had concerned friends, but she hated the appearance of this. If Michael himself knew the appearance of this, he didn't say so.

Reb made him a peanut butter and Fluff sandwich for

lunch, just the way he liked it, crusts peeled off instead of cut, but Michael didn't glance at it.

Midafternoon, their stepfather sat down on the curb next to him. If you had to have a stepfather, Kells was adequate. That was as far as Lily would go. He was not the sort of stepparent any of them had dreamed of. (If any kid dreams of stepparents.)

"I was thinking—" began Kells.

"He'll be here in a minute," said Michael fiercely.

Nobody had anything to say after that.

Lily thought, It will kill Michael if it doesn't happen.

She went back in the house and up to her room. She was skeptical of prayer, never paid attention at church and referred to the minister—Dr. Bordon—as Dr. Boring. But into the quiet air of her bedroom, she said, "God?"

He wasn't listening. Lily could tell. She spoke more sharply. "God, Michael needs this. Make it happen. Don't give me that stuff about free will, how people make their own choices, how your choices don't always intersect with the choices of others in a pleasing fashion and how responsibility lies with the individual. Get down here and make this happen."

He was listening now. Lily could tell that too. "Now!" she said fiercely to God.

At exactly that moment, Dad arrived.

Even Lily was impressed.

Into his end of the telephone, Michael whispered, "I'm at the airport, Lily. Dad drove."

Lily came quickly, easily and often to wrath, so she arrived at smoking fury instantly. In the same car, she thought, that he was driving two and a half weeks ago when he came ten hours late to get his own little boy, the little boy who begged to live with him. A car without room for a bike and fishing poles and ten boxes and two suitcases. "What do I have to do here?" Dad had said irritably. "Pay to ship this stuff? What is this stuff, anyway? Does it matter?"

"No," said Michael quickly. "None of it matters."

Kells had said in his bland pudgy way, "I think we can pack most of it if we're careful," and their father said, "Whatever," and Kells got everything except the bike and the fishing poles into the trunk and the backseat, and Michael didn't care; he didn't care about one thing except driving away with Dad. Michael could hardly even be bothered to say good-bye. Who were they, anyway? Sisters, mother, stepfather, half brother—so what?

Dad had come.

"Let me talk to Dad," said Lily.

"He isn't here."

"Where is he?"

"He left."

"What do you mean—left?"

"Don't tell," said Michael. "Promise you won't tell, Lily."

More of Lily's heart burned. Michael did not have secrets. Michael blatted everything to everybody; he was the sharing-est person out there.

Upstairs Nathaniel abandoned saying "Miikoooo" and returned to "Wiwwy." He was sobbing between syllables.

"I promise," said Lily.

"He was mad at me," said Michael, in a voice too soft and flat to be Michael's.

"But what's going on? Why are you at the airport? Where is Dad? Is he having a hard time parking the car?"

"I don't think he parked."

"Where is he, then?"

"I think he went back to his house."

"But who's with you?"

"Nobody," said Michael.

"You're alone at the airport?" she said, unable to believe it.

"Don't tell, Lily," said her brother. "I don't want anybody to know. Just come and get me."

"You're eight years old and he—" Lily didn't finish the sentence out loud—he threw you out on the sidewalk like a paper coffee cup? If she took a deep enough breath, the oxygen in her lungs would ignite. She would go up in smoke. That worthless lowlife pretend father! How dare he! I'll kill him, Lily decided. I'll have him arrested and jailed and tortured to death.

"It was my fault, Lily. Don't tell anybody. Especially Mom or Kells. Promise. You have to promise."

"I promise," she said, although she could not imagine how this could be kept a secret. But to keep it a secret, she couldn't ask a neighbor to drive her to LaGuardia. It wouldn't be too hard to get there by bus. She'd never done it, but people did. She could get the details from LaGuardia's Web site. Nate loved the bus, he'd be good. Driving herself wasn't a choice; Lily wasn't old enough to get a learner's permit, never mind weave her way to LaGuardia.

"You're coming?" said Michael. She could hear the pace of his breathing stepping up again, getting too fast and too shallow and very close to sobbing again.

Okay, she thought, planning hard. Nate and I get the bus, meet the plane, bring Michael home, put sheets on his old bed, get York settled underneath it. When Mom and Kells get here, *they'll* decide how to kill Dad. "What airline is your ticket?" she asked.

"I don't have a ticket," said Michael.

*chapter
2*

Michael. Age eight. Alone at Baltimore/Washington International Airport without a ticket?

"Do you have York?" she asked.

"I don't have anything. I didn't know what was going to happen. I didn't pack."

When Mom finds out, she'll bring in the FBI and ten lawyers, thought Lily.

Mom was a nice, good-humored person, but her post-divorce anger rose easily to the surface and she would take advantage of this. She'd bypass Michael for this huge and lovely chance to get even. She would get Dad jailed.

You would think there could be nothing worse than being abandoned by your father. But there was something worse. If bad things happened to his father, that eight-year-old would hold himself responsible. Michael would tumble and smash like the loser in some horrible Chutes and Ladders game.

But he could not stay alone in an airport. Anything could happen, something really hideously terrible. "Flag down a cop, Michael. There have to be dozens wandering around an airport."

"No."

"I'll talk to them. You don't have to."

"No!"

What if the police kept Michael? Some judge in Maryland might put Michael in a foster home or some halfway house with real criminals. And how long would they keep him? Maybe not just overnight. Maybe weeks or months. And what if some sick and twisted judge—because according to the news, the world was full of them—decided Michael still belonged with Dad?

Because to the judge, Dad might claim it was just a mis-understanding.

And maybe it was.

Lily would keep Michael on this line and use her cell to call Dad. Dad would have an explanation.

"Are you still there?" Michael's voice was shaky.

Who cares about an explanation? Lily thought. What he'd better have is a plane ticket. "I'm here. I'm telephoning Dad. You stay on the line while I get my cell. You know what, Michael? Maybe on his way to the parking lot Dad had a fender bender. Because he didn't mean for you to be alone, Michael. It was careless of him to drop you off, but he thought he'd be back in a second."

"He's not parking the car, Lily. He told me I'm not the son he had in mind. And then he drove away."

* * *

A hand landed on Michael's shoulder. A voice said, "You okay?"

Michael had been wholly absorbed by his sister's voice and the background music of Nathaniel screaming his name. He'd pressed his face into the silvery chrome of the phone box, getting closer to Lily. So rarely had Michael cried in his life that for a moment he couldn't figure out how his face had gotten all wet.

The man bending over him must be a pilot; blue uniform with several insignia including wings. Michael wiped away the tears with the back of his hand. "Sure, I'm okay," he said. "Just saying good-bye to my sister."

"Airports are all about saying good-bye," agreed the pilot. "But who's with you, son? I don't see anybody in the whole room."

He was right. There were no longer kids playing, or parents watching, or a couple kissing by the window. Michael was alone. Post-9/11, airports hated anything unusual. Michael couldn't stop being eight and he couldn't stop being alone, but he could stop crying and he could fake a family. He dragged out the grandmother excuse again.

"Tell you what," said the pilot. "I'll just wait with you till she comes."

"What's going on?" Lily demanded through the phone.

"A pilot wants to sit with me until Grandma gets back from the bathroom," said Michael.

"Let me talk to him."

"No."

"Michael, you can't be alone in an airport."

"I am, though. Go get Nathaniel out of his crib. He's crying too hard. He might choke."

"We should be so lucky. Okay, I'm going upstairs to get Nate. But you stay on the line. I'm on the portable phone and I'm carrying you with me."

The pilot slouched against the wall as if he planned to stay for years.

"You remember your promise?" Michael asked her.

"I remember."

"Say it back to me."

"I promise not to tell," said Lily.

I should never have told her anything, thought Michael. She knows what Dad said and what he did and she'll tell. If she does, I'm going to tell everybody she's making it up.

I'm never going to repeat it to anybody again. I'm never going to have tears on my face again either. I'm going to grow up right now and get it over with.

Michael took a long slow breath, had some long slow thoughts, and got it over with.

"Bye, Lily," he said, hanging up on her. "There's Grandma!" he said to the pilot. "Thanks for waiting with me!" He crossed the carpet, passed some flight monitors and arrived at the side of two elderly women, who weren't together, just near each other. One woman was balancing a huge carry-on bag, a huge purse and a huge coat. "It's summer," Michael said to her. "Really hot out. How come you have such a heavy coat?"

She beamed at him. "I'm going to Russia and Finland! Isn't that exciting? And September in those countries might be cold."

Michael had only the vaguest idea where Russia and

Finland might be. "I wish I could go too," he said, which was certainly true.

* * *

Sobbing until his nose and eyes were equally drippy, Nathaniel had gotten yuck all over his hands and face. His diaper was full. Lily handled him with grim efficiency. Then she put him in a fresh T-shirt and shorts that matched and even located the right socks, so he was bright blue with white trim and red sailboats. She yanked apart the Velcro on his little sneakers, fastened them tight and carried him downstairs. Nate hated being carried downstairs. He liked bumping down on his padded bottom.

In the kitchen she filled a sippy cup with milk and handed it over.

She could not believe Michael had hung up on her. She *really* could not believe that she was the one who had to call Dad and demand action. If anything had ever been Mom's job, this was it. Lily would rather skewer Dad for barbecue than talk to him.

"Wiwwy okay?" asked Nathaniel anxiously.

Her little brother was not yet two years old and he was worried.

How come Dad wasn't worried? How could he have driven away? No parent would do that!

And surely their father, their own biological, chemical, neurological blood father, surely Dennis Rosetti had not said out loud to his little boy: You're not the son I had in mind.

Lily crushed Nathaniel in the hug she could not give Michael. Then she strapped him into his high chair and gave him a Fig Newton. He liked to peel away the cookie part and mash the fruit part and, when the tray was a disgusting mat of crumb, jam and smear, put his face down and lick it up. Michael encouraged this style of eating.

After he left to live with Dad, Michael had not called home every day. He hadn't called every second or third day. They had to call him and he never had anything to say. It was unlike Michael to have nothing to say.

School had started a week earlier for Michael down there than it had up here. Michael wasn't willing to discuss school, either. Michael was average in class, struggling with reading, worried by arithmetic, but still, he loved school. He loved the other kids and the teachers and the teams and the activities. Reb used to sit with him, reading aloud the sports section in the newspaper for reading practice, using her finger to follow the lines of print because Michael was embarrassed to use his finger.

Lily had accidentally left the portable phone in the crib upstairs. She called Dad on her cell. Her hands were so swollen with rage that her fingertips barely fit on the tiny buttons. On the fourth ring, he answered it, his voice relaxed. "Hey, Lils," he said, knowing her from his caller ID.

She could see him perfectly: handsome and lean, with a tousled casual look on which he spent a lot of time. Loafers without socks, sunglasses hooked on his shirt, always a jacket but never a tie. Very blue eyes, so he looked like a sled dog. He was in marketing. He could sell anybody anything.

"Tell me," said Lily fiercely, "that you did not drop Michael off at the airport without a ticket."

"Let Kells buy the ticket."

"What does Kells have to do with it?" she yelled. Her fury filled the room and oozed down the hall and up the stairs. Nathaniel wasn't touching his cookie. He was staring at her in fear. "Did you tell Michael he isn't the son you had in mind?"

"He isn't."

"How dare you!"

"It was an experiment, Lily. It didn't work."

"He's your son, not an experiment!"

"Whatever."

She tried to calm herself but nothing came of it. "What happened?" she screamed.

"He was a hell of a lot of work for very little return," said her father. "I've been trying to find my own space for a long time now, and if there's one thing I've learned, it's not to pour myself into fruitless ventures."

As simple as that. Little boys took time and attention. Money and effort. A man could be doing more interesting things. So Dad could stay casual and handsome and blond, while Michael had to carry this with him all his life: He was worth nothing to his own father.

"I hate you!" Lily screamed into the phone. "You are not a father!"

"Oh, cut the drama."

"I will never use that word 'father' again, Dennis Rosetti! I will never *refer* to you again. I will never *speak* to you again."

Dennis Rosetti laughed.

Lily flung her cell phone against the wall. It didn't get damaged. She smashed it to the floor and stomped on it and when she was done she got Nathaniel out of his high chair and held him tight and rocked him and they both sobbed, she in fury and he in fear, and the regular phone rang.

"It's me," said Michael cheerfully. "I've found a great spot to hang out. There's this group of high school kids waiting for their flight, and it's late, and they're lying on the carpet and playing cards and computer games. I'm blending in. There are phones everywhere once you really look, Lily. When are you getting here?"

When was Lily getting where? To BWI? How could she possibly do that?

The faith in Michael's voice was like religion, the religion possessed by their grandmother, who never missed church, who believed completely and without any fretting. God is good, she would say, and that seemed to be all she needed.

Michael's faith that Lily would come was so complete that Lily got faith too and immediately had a plan.

When Reb had received her college acceptance, she had also gotten dozens of credit cards in the mail. With Mom's permission, Reb had activated one, and Mom and Kells talked often about the responsibility of a credit line and what should or should not be charged.

Lily had done a wrong thing. She had taken one of the cards and activated it herself, picking 3000 for a PIN number, since somebody ought to be using it. So Lily had a credit card in Reb's name. Lily could charge a plane ticket. In some circles, this would be called credit card fraud.

If Lily got the bill when it came in the mail, and neither Mom nor Kells ever saw it, and she paid it off out of her savings account, she could actually buy Michael's ticket for him. One good thing about the divorce—the children got Christmas and birthday checks from three sets of grandparents. Reb spent hers on big-ticket items like a kayak. Michael frittered his away on little things like popcorn at the movies. Lily put hers in the bank.

"Here's what we do," she said to Michael. "I phone the airlines. I get you an e-ticket. You fly back alone. Kids fly alone all the time. It'll be an adventure. Meanwhile, Nate and I grab a bus to LaGuardia and meet you. We'll be back home long before Mom and Kells are back from Reb's college. While you wait for me to make my calls, get something to eat." This was because Michael didn't waste time on meals (all that sitting around) and ate just enough to take the edge off, which meant he was starving to death ten minutes later. "Have a Happy Meal," she ordered him, "and call me back in twenty minutes."

"I don't have any money."

Lily no longer believed any of this. She summarized the situation, because she must have gotten it wrong. "He opened the car door and drove away? And didn't give you even a dollar? Or a ticket? Or let you pack York?"

Lily had ripped off his cheerful front by mentioning York. Michael let out one jagged weep.

"It's okay," said Lily quickly. "I'll call Dad and tell him to airmail York right now. I won't let him do anything to York."

She had just resolved never to speak to the snake again, or admit that he even existed, and now she had to call and beg. She couldn't wait, because a man willing to throw out his kid would drive straight home to throw out the stuffed bear.

Nathaniel was beginning to cry now too. He hated raised voices, which he rarely heard and which frightened him. Lily shoved the high chair next to the refrigerator. Nate loved to peel the magnets off.

"Don't call Dad," said Michael urgently.

"He's got York, though," Lily pointed out.

"Lily?" whispered Michael.

"Yes?" she whispered back.

"Dad threw York out the first night. He made me watch the garbagemen take him in the morning. He said I had to grow up."

Lily felt herself growing up with such speed she might

have swallowed a magic potion. "Okay," she said. "It's a deal. I promise. I don't call Dad. I don't call Mom. I get you a ticket, you fly home, I pick you up. Call me back in twenty minutes so I can tell you about your ticket. If I don't hear from you, I will call the airport police myself. Got it?"

"Got it," said Michael, and once more, his voice was full of faith.

Faith in Lily.

chapter 3

"You can't buy a ticket at your end," said the airline clerk, "and have a little boy use it at his end. An eight-year-old is permitted to travel alone, but his parent or guardian has to sign him in. He can't pick it up at the ticket counter himself! Anyway, how would an eight-year-old get to the airport alone?"

"Good point," said Lily. "Have a good day," she added before she hung up, because somebody might as well have a good day. I can't get Michael a ticket, she thought.

"Wiwwy?" shouted Nathaniel.

"I'm right here."

Nathaniel came around the corner, thrilled as always to

find her on the other side of a wall. "Michael's on the other side of a wall, too," she told him.

Nate beamed at the mention of Michael. "Okie, Wiwwy," he said happily.

Another brother with complete faith in Lily.

Her mother, now, did not have complete faith in Lily. Mom was always worried that Lily would make some massive mistake, or a series of minor mistakes that would add up to a massive mistake, so Mom was always giving detailed instructions to prevent this from happening. Her mother was going to be justified.

Mom would just splatter this story everywhere.

It was the kind of thing Mom and her support group loved to talk about. It nagged at Kells that he had been married to her for three and a half years and still she went once a month to her divorce support group. But even that wouldn't be enough telling for Mom. Next she'd tell Michael's classroom teachers, so that they could "intervene"—a favorite pastime of teachers.

Perhaps Michael would be sent to a therapist. Maybe Lily, too.

Michael would be in one room playing with action figures, his psychiatrist watching to see if Michael ripped the heads off the grown-men dolls. Lily would be in the next room with colored pencils, her psychiatrist expecting Lily to draw a family with a dead father, the corpse studded with knives she had thrown.

Lily pressed Nate's hot little body against her eyes so his cute little sailboat shirt would soak up her tears.

The grown-ups would want Michael to "get past" this event, and they'd make him talk for years in therapy. But who could "get past" a thing like that? A thing like that was always present.

Lily had never been to a therapist or a group session or a support group or even a guidance counselor. The closest she had ever come was church, where Dr. Bordon's sermons frequently dealt with the pain we all carry and how to handle it with the Lord's help. Lily's theory was that she would be in less pain if he skipped the sermon. Or at least condensed it. She would look at the congregation around her and think, Nobody here is in pain. They're having the time of their lives. You can't buy a house in this zip code unless you make more money than God anyway. The people here do have everything.

Mom might even tell Dr. Bordon about Dad's airport choices. Lily and Michael would have to sit in his study and pray, for heaven's sake.

Nathaniel was getting twitchy. Lily set him free and he took off, eager to explore the downstairs, as if he had not just seen it prior to naptime, and every single other day for twenty-two months.

Meanwhile, Michael would have to face Jamie, his best friend. Jamie lived two miles away. What an event in Michael's life when Mom said he could ride his bike to Jamie's. Jamie's mother said she was never letting *her* son take such risks. Michael loved that ride, always hoping it would turn out to be risky, but it never did.

When Michael had made up his mind to live with his dad, he hadn't cared about Jamie any more than last month's weather. He was going to have a real dad. But now the whole town would know what kind of father Dennis Rosetti had turned out to be—and plenty of them would always wonder what kind of flaw the little boy must have, to be discarded like that.

Lily was so puffy and spongy with rage she thought she must look like somebody on chemo.

If Michael can't fly up here by himself, she decided, I'll fly down and get him.

She needed picture ID. She didn't have any. She rummaged in Mom's horribly messy desk until she located Reb's passport, which had been obtained for a class trip to Spain when Reb was sixteen.

I look a lot like her, thought Lily. Same hair, same eyes. "Hi," said Lily to a pretend ticket agent. "I'm Reb Rosetti."

"Reb Rosetti" sounded like a mud wrestler. No wonder her sister planned to be Rebecca from now on.

"Good afternoon," she practiced. "I'm Rebecca Rosetti!"

What did they do to people who falsified their identities at airports? Nothing good.

If they caught her, she'd probably be responsible for ten delayed flights and possibly an airport evacuation. But how would they catch her? They didn't know there was somebody named Lily, so they wouldn't wonder if she was Lily masquerading as Reb.

It was half past twelve. Mom and Kells and Reb were probably halfway to Rochester. This was also in New York State, but Lily tended to think of New York in three parts: New York City, the suburbs and the rest of the state—an unknown hinterland in which anything could happen and where nobody went except on weekends.

"Wook, Wiwwy!" cried Nathaniel, triumphantly holding Mom's cell phone. Lily swiftly substituted the television remote and Nate searched joyfully for Volume Control. "What am I supposed to do with you during this rescue?" she said to him.

"Watch TV," said Nathaniel, happily clicking.

Lily got on the kitchen computer and went to the travel site bookmarked by Kells, who bought his business tickets online. She filled in the right blanks. The choices were few.

There was exactly one flight nonstop to Baltimore and it was leaving in two hours. The return trips—every one of them—involved detours to Raleigh or Atlanta or Boston. She was furious. "This is New York!" she yelled. "You ought to be able to fly nonstop to New York from any place!"

It took seven minutes to use the fraudulent credit card to buy the tickets, and even though Nathaniel, if he sat on her lap, didn't need a ticket, it cost a fortune. Fifteen years old and bankrupt, she thought.

At the LaGuardia Web site she got directions for public transportation. Then she studied her cash position. She personally had eight dollars. She emptied the jar where Mom threw one-dollar bills and change, and found two twenties in the middle, which was excellent. But she didn't dare take a taxi. It could easily be twenty dollars, and she might need that cash. Buses were okay, just slow. There wasn't a moment to waste. She stuffed the baby's insulated tote bag with diapers, juice boxes and a Baggie of Cheerios.

Would airport security notice that the two-year-old called her Wiwwy instead of Reb? Would they ask why she bought the tickets minutes before departure? Would they wonder why she had no luggage?

* * *

Michael was fine until the delayed flight of the schoolkids around him was suddenly boarding and the kids were leaping up, tossing their stuff into backpacks and discarding leftover snacks.

Michael was so hungry he almost asked a girl if he could eat her pizza crust. She threw it into a wastebasket, the kind with small round holes in the top. Michael stood on tiptoe to see if he could reach the crust, but he couldn't.

And then he was alone.

He walked purposefully for a few steps, as if he had a destination, but he was approaching security, which wasn't good, so he swerved toward the men's room, pausing for a sip at the drinking fountain. He had no watch but he could see the digital time on one of the many monitors in the building. Okay, he told himself. Four more minutes and I can call Lily back.

His little brother said okay all the time. "Okie, Miikoooo" was what Nathaniel actually said. If Michael shouted "Leave me alone!" or "Don't touch my stuff!" or "Shut up!" Nathaniel said meekly, "Okie, Miikoooo."

Nathaniel loved Michael.

That had been its own reason to leave: the suffocating, maddening love of Nathaniel. How could one person, especially such a small person, repeat the same name so often in one day, play the same stupid game, mash the same cookie, hug the same hug, joyfully greet that same brother?

Nathaniel made him crazy.

But now Michael knew what it was *not* to be loved.

Nate, I promise, thought Michael. I won't have better things to do when I get home.

Although he knew he would. Two days home—two hours—given how annoying Nate was, possibly two minutes—and Michael would be sick of him again.

Several men were leaning on the wall next to the ladies' room, waiting for their wives, so Michael leaned there too, and slid slowly down the wall until he was cross-legged on the gray carpet.

When he glanced up again, a whole new set of men was leaning against the wall.

And he had killed the four minutes and now he could phone. He ran all the way to the wall of phones near the playroom.

He was too excited to pay attention and got the digits wrong, and the call didn't go through. He tried again and got the digits wrong this time too. His hands got cold and the back of his eyes hurt. What if he had forgotten the numbers? What if he couldn't reach Lily after all? What if—

Slowly, carefully, he tried a third time.

"You're one minute early," said his sister.

Michael wanted to gallop through the phone line to be with her. "Hi."

"Here's the deal. I can't just get you an e-ticket and have you pick it up at the gate because you're a kid and they don't let kids do that."

Michael's heart sank.

"So Nate and I are coming for you. We're taking a flight out of LaGuardia at two-forty. We land at BWI at three-fifty-one. Then all three of us fly home together. I'm going as Reb because I'm using her passport for ID, so you have to call me Reb. Whoever picks you up has to be a grown-up, so I'm eighteen. Don't forget that. But you're coming as you and Nate is going as himself."

"Like spies," said Michael.

"Exactly. Now, remember that spies get shot if they're caught. So don't goof this up."

Michael was overwhelmed with horror. On TV news there was always a city in a distant country where people shot each other or blew each other up. He couldn't catch his breath, thinking of Lily getting shot.

"Joke," said his sister. "We aren't spies, nobody gets shot."

"Oh."

"Keep phoning me. Not this phone. My cell. You know my cell phone number by heart?"

"I know it by heart," said Michael, and his heart actually hurt, pierced by the numbers of his sister's phone, as if those numbers had bitten him.

"Meet us at the baggage claim. Do you know where that is?"

"No."

"You have till three-fifty-one to find it. It's twelve-fifteen. Can you manage almost four hours?"

Four hours. Michael was stunned. He had hardly managed twenty minutes. Where was he going to sit for four hours? "Yes," he said.

"If airport security does pick you up, be polite. Tell them your eighteen-year-old sister Reb is on her way. Tell them what plane. Tell them you don't know how things got messed up but Reb will solve things. Give them my cell number."

"Okay. What will they do then?"

"Nothing," said Lily. "I'll still land and we'll still fly home."

Reb could lie like a rug; she was the best fibber there'd ever been. But Lily was like Michael. Lies were so much trouble that she generally told the truth and accepted the consequences. He knew when Lily was telling a lie because her voice got forceful and loud, as if she was shoving it into being real.

If security found Michael, it would not be all right.

They might not fly home.

Lily flung on makeup. She fastened her hair the way Reb had it in the passport picture. Lily despised pink, but Reb wore it all the time and she had worn it for her passport photo. Lily grabbed silvery pink cotton pants Reb had once given her and filched an expensive short-sleeved pink shirt of her mother's, tying a thin, lacy white sweater around her waist in case the air-conditioning was freezing. She looked as close to eighteen as she was going to get.

She stuck a new box of playing cards in with the Cheerios. Nate loved cards. He chewed them, bent them, ripped them, stacked them, threw them. She double-checked her credit card and Reb's passport, stuck the cell phone in her purse and they set out.

Nate loved the bus and everybody on it. He stood on his seat, holding her shoulder or hair to steady himself, and he studied everything and talked to everyone.

Lily's thoughts leaped and sputtered like a fire being doused with water. Michael, be safe, she thought. God, keep Michael safe, she ordered Him.

She couldn't tell if He was listening.

* * *

The ticket agent took Reb's passport and the piece of paper on which Lily had written her ticket confirmation number, glancing so briefly at Lily it could have been a blink. Kells had said once that people were busy thinking about themselves, and even when it was their job to think about you, they were probably still thinking about themselves. He seemed to be right.

Lily lifted Nathaniel onto the high counter so he wouldn't

jump up and down around her ankles calling, "Wiwwy! Wemme see too!"

The attendant asked her the routine questions without making eye contact. Perhaps she was allergic to toddlers, a tendency Lily could certainly understand.

Had Lily left her luggage unattended? No.

Had anybody unknown to her given her something to carry? No.

"Checking any luggage today?"

"No, thank you."

"Here's your boarding pass. Your row is empty at this moment. If you're lucky, nobody will sit there, and then your little brother gets his own seat. If you're not lucky, he sits on your lap the whole flight."

And that was it.

I really must look eighteen, she thought. Awesome. Always wanted to be eighteen. Always wanted to be Reb.

At the security barriers, the guards wanted Nathaniel to walk through by himself, but he was having none of it and had to be peeled off her. Then Lily walked through while Nathaniel sobbed in panic and then the torture was over and she could cuddle him while the guards patted him on the back and told him what a brave boy he was.

They had a few minutes to spare, so she let Nathaniel walk, and he cried out in wonder at all the exciting things. The best was a big soft pretzel dipped in cinnamon sugar. Instantly, even though she just gave him a crumb, Nathaniel was smeared head to toe with sugar and butter.

Probably the best explanation to give Mom and Kells for the sudden reappearance of Michael was the simplest: Michael didn't like it there after all. It wouldn't occur to them that Dad hadn't bought Michael a ticket—how could that occur to anybody? Mom wouldn't be thrilled that Lily had taken Nate on public transportation to LaGuardia, and she'd complain that Lily ought to have called neighbors to drive her, but with any luck, Mom would be so pleased to find out Michael had decided *her* house was better than *his* house that she wouldn't press it.

It would be a real kick in the face if Dad was the one who spilled the facts—which he might, because he didn't even care, and Mom was bound to call. Lily would e-mail him. His address was "denrose"—a good name for him, now that she could never use the word "Dad" or the word "father" again.

At the gate, Lily thought: I haven't heard from Michael since we left home to catch the bus. He has to call me; I can't call him.

She whipped out her cell phone.

It wasn't hers.

She had smashed her cell to pieces.

She had Mom's phone.

Michael could call all day and nobody would ever answer.

chapter 4

The night before he left to go live with his father, Michael had set two alarms to make sure he did not oversleep, into which he had put new batteries to make sure they did not fail. He also wore his watch to bed, and from twelve-thirty in the morning until four-thirty, he watched the glowing digital numbers change.

Now, in the airport, he did not know what he had been expecting when he lay awake all night long. Whatever it was, it had not existed, and Michael was filled with dread at what stretched ahead.

So many things he could not ward off.

Like Jamie.

Jamie worshipped his own dad, who ran the town soccer

program when he wasn't running his company, which delivered heating oil. Jamie got to help repair engines and fix furnaces and his dad played every ball game with Jamie, or took him to one. Since Jamie's dad was perfect, Jamie had explained that Michael's dad too would be perfect, and that going to live with him was a perfect idea.

Michael would never betray his father. He decided never to talk to Jamie again so that Jamie would not suspect.

Michael slid into the midst of some young men who stood in a long ticket line. They never looked down to where Michael was. For eleven minutes he was safe. Then an airline attendant began working her way down the line, examining each ticket and making sure the person was in the right line.

She got closer. She was heavy, very black, with complex braids. She was stern with people, but nice about it. Michael almost said to her, "I don't have a ticket. I don't have anything," because she would make it better. But it wouldn't be better for Dad.

Grown-ups got into deep and serious trouble when they left kids on their own. There had been this woman who left her two little kids in car seats while she went into the grocery for a gallon of milk, and she was gone five minutes, and got charged with child abuse.

Of course, her kids had been babies.

Michael was no baby.

Still.

If I can get home, he thought, nobody will know Dad did anything wrong.

Especially not Mom, who in some terrible divorce way would rejoice. See? I was right! she would say. Kells would not say any such thing. Kells stuck to subjects like baseball and dinner.

It came to Michael that his stepfather was a better person than his real father.

He could not allow such a thing to be said. He could not permit a comparison. The ticket agent got closer, so Michael slid out of line and went back to the play area.

He passed a gift shop selling stuffed animals. They were colorful: monkeys in lime green and puppies in orange. He thought of York in a landfill. Filthy broken things thrown on top of York to stain and crush him. Michael wished he had gone to the landfill with York. It wouldn't be any different, and at least he'd have York to hold.

He picked up a newspaper somebody'd left on a bench and felt slightly better. Every single person at the airport was carrying something, and now Michael was carrying something too. He fit in.

He tried the stairs and found an observation room, where he sat for quite a while, nose pressed to the window, watching Southwest planes come and go.

The four hours seemed a forever thing, his heart and soul suspended like a plane.

Nathaniel was so perfect on board the plane that Lily could have sold him for enough money to pay for the tickets.

The flight attendants adored him.

The lady across the aisle played his favorite card game, where Nathaniel threw the card on the floor and the other person picked it up.

The man in the seat directly behind them shook hands with Nate about six hundred times through the crack in the seats and each time, Nate burst into giggles of joy.

"What's the fun part?" asked another passenger, after about a hundred times.

"Who knows?" said the guy. "He sure likes shaking hands, though."

"Is he bothering you?" asked Lily, who knew perfectly well that Nate was bothering him; that was all Nate did—bother people.

But the man just laughed. "It's a short flight," he said.

Lily had run into enough kind people to staff a hotel. How come her very own father wasn't one of them?

Her heart was pounding faster and faster, as if she were turning into a hummingbird. Michael could not call her. He had had complete faith in her, and now she too had abandoned him at the airport. Three times she'd called that pay phone Michael had used. Nobody answered the first time, a stranger answered the second time and nobody the third time.

Nate tucked himself up in her lap and ate Cheerios one at a time, curling his stubby fingers carefully around a Cheerio and squishing it into Cheerio dust just before he put it on his tongue.

"Gonna get Miikooo?" he said fifty times.

"Going to get Michael," she agreed fifty times. Half the Cheerios got dropped on the floor. Lily needed to conserve snacks, so she picked them up and stuffed them back in the bag.

I don't want to save denrose with excuses, she thought. I want him to be punished! I want him to suffer. I want him to end up in the meanest, roughest jail in the world. One with snakes and rats and cholera.

Enraged, she was panting like a dog in summer.

How dare you? she thought. How dare you?

* * *

Michael's need to talk to Lily almost tripped him, like an invisible wire strung across the corridor. But no matter how calm he tried to be, no matter how carefully he tried to press the right numbers, he couldn't make the call.

I told Lily I had her number by heart, he thought. But I don't.

The list of things he had done wrong seemed so long. Michael could not see how he could go on. Or why. What was he worth, anyway?

Nothing to Dad.

Michael tried the phone number at other phones in other locations. He never got the numbers right.

Darkness enveloped Michael. He had no thoughts to go with it. He thought he would fall down, but there were still things to do: he had to cover for Dad. Nobody must know or see or guess.

The darkness became deeper. He could hardly keep his eyes open from the suffocating pressure of it.

I didn't grow up, he thought. That was the problem. Dad is right. I have to grow up. Right now.

Instead, he had an odd enticing vision of those open girders high above the ticket counters. He saw himself balancing there for a moment, and then letting go on purpose.

* * *

Nate picked out a Cheerio and gave it to the guy who had been shaking his hand.

"I especially like the lint on your Cheerio," said the guy's seatmate.

"Eat it!" demanded Nate.

In an act of true love, the guy ate it.

* * *

Around the third hour, Michael remembered that he had to find the luggage carousels because he was meeting Lily at Baggage Claim. How could he have wasted all this time without finding Baggage Claim?

It took forever to locate the escalators down. He was sick with fear that he had missed her. He hadn't had his watch on when they left so fast in the morning, so he had to check the time on the flight monitors, and the complexity of the information up there made the clock part hard to find.

The carousels were motionless. Security guards stood there anyway, also motionless, frozen until they were needed.

Michael trudged along car rental counters and past free hotel phones. There were lots of brochures for places to go and things to do. Michael took every one he could reach. He hated reading, but he could take his brochures back to the toy yellow and blue plane, curl up under a seat, and look at pictures.

"Passenger MacArthur, Passenger MacArthur," said an overhead voice. "Meet your party at the information booth at Baggage Claim."

That was where Michael was.

Two middle-aged women were definitely the ones worried about Passenger MacArthur. They bobbed up and down, peering this way and that. It was several minutes before

Passenger MacArthur appeared, and Michael was aston-ished to see another little chubby middle-aged woman. Passenger MacArthur had sounded like a dad to him.

I could have Dad paged, he thought.

The three women hugged and cried, "It's so good to see you!" and "The car's in short-term parking, not much of a walk," so Michael walked with them.

I thought we would play catch, thought Michael. I thought we would be outside in his yard and play catch.

He clung to his brochures.

The garage was a cavern, like a sunken Japanese car dealership, hundreds of black four-door sedans lined up between great concrete pillars and tiny glowing Exit signs. Michael went over a few aisles where the shadows were thicker. He turned around and could no longer see where he'd come in, and when he tried to find the terminal, it wasn't there, and when he found a door, it led in some other direction entirely, and when he ran back to the four-door sedans, there were none. Only huge SUVs brushing side-view mirrors with the next SUV.

* * *

When they finally landed, Nathaniel was exhausted. He desperately needed a nap. Lily had no stroller. She was going to have to carry him and hope he slept against her shoulder. She felt very thin, as if her slamming heart had made her lose weight, and lose brain capacity, and lose hope.

It had been four hours since she talked to Michael.

Nathaniel began to cry that infuriating whine of little kids who should be asleep.

He was unbearably heavy.

She thought of the word "unbearably" and wondered if "bear" was inside it.

Bears. York.

She was filled with fear.

She could think of a thousand terrible things that could have happened to Michael during these hours of silence. Things much worse than what Dad had done.

The flow of people carried Lily along. She didn't have to make choices. Everybody else knew where to go. They paraded to the baggage claim, where Michael should be.

But there was no Michael.

chapter 5

Michael woke up. He was sleeping on a mattress of travel brochures, deep inside the wooden play plane. Lily! he thought. When is she coming? What time is it? I have to get to the baggage claim!

He crawled out and ran into the terminal—read the time on a monitor.

It was 4:12.

Lily had landed more than fifteen minutes ago. He had missed her! What if she'd given up and gone home? Where was the escalator? He had to find Baggage Claim.

It seemed to Michael that hundreds of people—tall people, fat people, white people, black people, uniformed people, old people—stared at him and pointed at him. He fled and threw up in a men's room.

He hadn't eaten in so long there was nothing to throw up, and the acid burned his throat.

When he left the bathroom, he had to walk with his fingertips brushing the wall to steady himself.

He had to find those escalators. He stumbled past the gift shop, but it was not the gift shop he remembered. It had stuffed animals on display, but different ones. I'm lost, he thought. I missed Lily's plane and I'm in the wrong place.

The gift shop was entirely open to the hall, and right in front was a little display wagon filled with teddy bears. One of them looked a little like York. Michael could not help touching its pitching arm, and then he could not help lifting it out of the rack, and then he could not help hugging it.

A woman yelled at him from her cash register. "Hey!" she yelled. "You stealing that?"

"I'm just holding it," he whispered.

The woman stomped over to him.

A security guard stomped over to him.

Michael could not seem to stop holding the bear. He could not seem to give it back to the woman.

"What's your name, son?" said the officer.

I'm not a son, thought Michael. Sons have fathers.

The woman folded her arms and glared at Michael while the officer said, "Where are your parents?"

He remembered Baggage Claim, the absolute necessity to get there. His head throbbed, the phone number that he had learned wrong hammering inside his head. I'm a thief, he thought. My father doesn't want me. I don't have York. "I'm waiting for my sister," he said weakly, and he looked down the great concourse as if she would be there and he saw that not only were the passengers and the crews and the workers and the guards rushing to meet planes, they were all pausing to stare at him, the little boy caught shoplifting.

From far away came a voice as high and clear as a piccolo. "Miikooooo! Miikooooo!"

Hurtling among knees and suitcases came his little brother, legs churning, arms out. Michael set the stolen bear on the little wagon and went to his knees and Nathaniel flung himself on Michael and Michael knew what it was to be loved completely and without judgment and without thought or knowledge.

Lily was screaming at him from down the hallway. "I was on time!" she yelled. "I was *here*! I couldn't *find* you! I thought you were lost! I thought something awful happened! Where have you been! What are you doing! How could you scare me like that?"

Lily was as tall as the policeman. In only two and a half weeks, Michael had lost track of stuff like that. She looked old and angry. She had Nathaniel's tote bag and Michael thought, Bet she's got food. He was suddenly starving to death.

"Your brother was stealing this bear," said the stuffed animal woman.

"I was just holding it," he told Lily. "I held it too long. Lily, I didn't—"

"We'll buy the bear," said his sister to the woman. "I'm sorry he upset you. He was wrong. All of us are wrong. I even gave him the wrong cell phone number so he couldn't let me know what was happening. It's my fault. How much does the bear cost?"

"Oh, forget it," said the woman, irritably. "Just go! He didn't hurt the bear. I can still sell it."

"*I* wanna bear," said Nathaniel hopefully.

★ ★ ★

Michael with a paper bag of fast food and Nathaniel with the bear (Lily figured one more charge on the credit card wouldn't make a difference) went separately through security and were the first to board. They stared out the window at Baltimore/Washington International Airport.

Nathaniel fell asleep in Michael's lap, chubby legs spread apart, face buried on Michael's skinny chest. His little mouth hung open. He wasn't swallowing in his sleep and Michael's chest was getting wet.

"What do we tell Mom?" whispered Michael.

Lily hated all this whispering, as if Michael's lungs had been dented. "You tell Mom you missed us," she suggested. "It wasn't any fun down there and you wanted us back." They both knew Michael had not missed them.

What a huge and awe-ful gift to a father: I'm yours. I'm all yours. I'm throwing everything away in order to be yours. And the father didn't notice. The father had better stuff to do. Toss the kid back. Will the kid make it home? Who knows? Who cares?

"I know what," said Michael. "I'm very sick. I'm going to lose all my hair and have brain surgery." Because it would be okay to be sad, pale and wasted if he had IV needles and visitors and a funeral.

"No," said Lily. "Mom would race you to the pediatrician's and he'd give you shots. That won't work. And we don't want a reason where Dad throws you out. We want one where you throw him out. Let's make Dad disgusting. That won't be hard. He is disgusting. You left because you found out that he kicks puppies. Shoots bald eagles. Leaves loaded guns around the house for eight-year-old boys to play with."

"No," said Michael.

"He stages fake car accidents to get insurance money. He's up all night on disgusting Internet sites. He deals drugs at elementary schools."

"No, no and no."

"He won't let you play baseball. He says it's too slow and he can't be bothered."

Michael flinched. "Yes," he whispered, even more softly. "Lily, I thought we would play catch."

Lily had not known that she could despise denrose even more.

How could Mom have married this man to start with? Mom—

Mom.

She'd probably been calling the house all day, leaving frantic messages, wondering where Lily and Nathaniel were. She might even have called Amanda to see if Lily had gone over there.

Lily and Amanda had been friends since they were six weeks old and placed in the same infant care. Lily and Amanda shopped together, did their hair together, took the same classes, texted hourly, over the years had taken ballet and flute and tennis together.

Lily had not thought of Amanda once today. Lily had forgotten the whole world except Michael. She wondered whether to tell Amanda any of this. For once, Lily had no idea what Amanda might say or do.

"I better phone Mom," she told Michael, "so she doesn't worry."

"What are you going to tell her?" said Michael anxiously.

"Lies."

Michael gripped her arm. How small and cold his fingers were. Whereas Lily was burning. She was a furnace. "I don't want to talk," Michael whispered. "Don't tell her I'm here."

Lily nodded. Since she had Mom's cell, she called Kells on his. "Hi, Kells, can I talk to Mom?" she said, hoping to brush right past her stepfather.

"Sure can," he said, always cheerful. It was good that somebody in the family had that attitude.

"Lily!" cried her mother. "Where are you?"

No need to respond to difficult questions. "Guess what. Michael's coming home."

"Michael's coming home?"

"Yup. I guess it didn't work out. When are you getting back? Do you like Reb's roommate? What's the campus like?"

"Michael's coming home?"

"Yup," said Lily. "Nathaniel and I are picking Michael up at the airport. Nate's sound asleep, he doesn't even know what's happening. Did Reb cry when you left her at her dorm or did she kick you out in ten seconds?"

"Lily! This is so wonderful! I'm so happy! He's coming home! This is— Oh, dear. I guess I should call your father." Mom hated talking to Dad. She had to gird herself for days to make a call.

"I handled it," said Lily. "I bet from now on you can skip phone calls. The occasional e-mail should do it."

"Michael's coming home," Mom repeated, as if in prayer. "What airline, Lily? When does the plane land? Oh, Lord, now I have to worry about plane crashes."

"I have to go, Mom," said Lily.

"Wait! Do you have any money? How are you getting back and forth?"

"I raided your desk drawers and stuff. Don't worry. Everything's under control. See you. Bye!" She hung up.

"You didn't tell any lies," said Michael, marveling.

The plane took off.

Lily fell into a useless, terrible sleep.

A dream crept up on her. It began with a smashed telephone, but in the horrid way of dreams, the phone kept getting up and throwing itself at Lily while her father's voice crawled out of it, like spiders. The phone stuck to her fingers and she couldn't peel it off. She ran through the dark web of an endless terminal filled with sneering gawking people while the phone clung to her fingers and a terrible roar filled her ears. The roar of the nightmare was her own voice, dragged up from such depths that her lungs bled.

You are not a father. I will never use that word "father" again.

★ ★ ★

When they finally got home, the house might have been some ancient sanctuary or temple. Lily wanted to be inside it as she had rarely wanted anything in her life.

In the front hall, she turned on the light and stood on the old strip of rug. The same old watercolor hung over the same narrow table, cluttered with the same old music and catalogs and library books and pencils and pieces off things.

All her life, Lily had yearned for a neat and tidy house, and never had she seen anything as welcoming as the chaos of home.

Because the dumb flight went south in order to go north, and because of a layover, even though Lily had spent her last dollars to hurry home in a taxi, it was almost midnight.

Nathaniel disintegrated into sobbing exhaustion. Ignoring him, she poked the messages on the answering machine.

Four from Mom. All earlier in the day, when she had not been able to reach Lily.

We're talking panic here, thought Lily, and remembered that she personally had not panicked.

There was no message from Dad.

Did my little boy get home okay? Tell him I'm sorry. Tell Lily I was wrong. Tell my kids I love them.

No. There were no messages like that.

Michael walked through each room of the house, staring, as if maybe in *that* room, he would understand.

Nathaniel moved from sobbing into screaming. Lily had the passing thought that if anybody should be abandoned at an airport, it was a cranky two-year-old.

"Wiwwy." Nathaniel chinned himself on the waistband of Lily's pink trousers.

Michael hoisted Nathaniel and kissed him. "Come on, Nate. I'll give you a bath. That'll make you feel better. Then we'll both go to bed. Remember how we share a bedroom?"

"Wiwwy come too," Nathaniel demanded.

"No," said Lily. "I'm taking a shower."

In her bathroom, she tried to wash the whole day down the drain, but she couldn't get it off her skin. She put on her summer pajamas and went to check on Michael and Nathaniel. They had tubbed together and were squeaky clean and wrinkled like prunes.

Still to come was Nathaniel crying himself to sleep.

Lily reminded herself that good sisters did not throw their little brothers down the cellar stairs but were patient.

Michael put Nathaniel in his crib and tucked a blanket around him. "Don't do any crying, Nate. You're too old. Grow up."

"Okie, Miikooo," said Nathaniel. He closed his eyes and went to sleep, a recruit taking orders from his sergeant.

Lily dragged herself downstairs, wrapped the smashed cell phone in old newspaper, as if it were particularly disgusting garbage, and even took it outside to the trash barrel and fastened the lid tightly.

The kitchen phone rang.

She tottered back in to answer.

"Darling?" cried her mother. "We're almost home! We're on the Whitestone Bridge! Did you get Michael? Is everything okay? Why didn't you call me? I'm a wreck! Is Michael all right?" Michael had run downstairs to signal yet again that he did not want to talk.

Lily did not know how she could do more to protect Michael. But protecting Michael had hardly begun. Lily could not let the school system have any idea what had happened. Was anything more vicious than a gossipy teacher? Yes.

A gossipy counselor.

Schools lived for that word "dysfunctional." It was right up there with the all-time favorite phrase "low self-esteem." Teachers loved to say to each other, "Little Michael comes from a dysfunctional family, you know. Predictable result. Low self-esteem." He'd be in Special Needs in a heartbeat. He'd spend his life with people whose idea of kindness was to rip open a wound every week, so it never healed, but bled in front of everybody. Lily had seen what the Self-Esteem crowd could do to a kid.

Perhaps counseling had its place. The problem was, it didn't keep its place. It spread like a virus, infecting a kid's whole school year, and creeping into the next year, and the next, invading every classroom and lodging in the mind of every teacher. Once said out loud, it would go with Michael all the days of his school life: divorce issues; abandoned by father; subsequent reading problems; low self-esteem; needs counseling.

"Michael's asleep, Mom," Lily told the teacher she loved most in the world. "And I'm asleep on my feet. We'll see you in the morning."

"Lily, I want details!"

"There aren't any details. And Mom, don't wake us up early tomorrow, okay?" Tomorrow was Sunday. Usually Lily complained about church, but this week it would serve a purpose. It would postpone conversation. "Wake us up with exactly enough time to get dressed," she said.

"First you'll need a sturdy breakfast."

Lily never needed a sturdy breakfast. Lily liked weak, fragile breakfasts—a sip of orange juice and a single blueberry pried out of a muffin. "See you in the morning," she said, and disconnected. With any luck, even at this hour, Mom and Kells would run into traffic and Lily really and truly would be asleep before they got home. She dragged herself upstairs, but the sleep that had flattened her on the plane did not come. She couldn't even get her eyes to close unless she weighted them with her hands. After a while, she got up and went into Michael and Nathaniel's room.

"I can't sleep either," Michael whispered.

She sat on the edge of his bed and they held each other in the dark.

chapter

6

Sunday morning, Mom kept flinging her arms around Michael and kissing him all over, the way she would kiss Nathaniel. "Oh, Michael! You just told your father you were coming home? Coming back to me? Oh, Michael, I'm so glad to see you! This is so wonderful!"

Michael slid out of her grasp and onto a chair, facing his glass of orange juice.

"Miikooo's home!" Nathaniel kept yelling. "Got Miikooo atta airport!"

"Yes, you did," said Kells. "You and your big sister went on a long taxi ride, didn't you?"

Nathaniel frowned. "No, Daddy. Went onna pane."

★ **65** ★

His father swung him in circles. "Michael went on the plane, didn't he? Did you see it land?"

"Michael, darling," said Mom, "I can't find your suitcases. Where are your things?"

Michael studied his orange juice.

"Once Michael decided to come back," said Lily, "there weren't many flights to choose from and there wasn't enough time for packing. Dad's going to ship his stuff." I, who hate him, she thought, am giving Dad an out.

"I think some drawers in your bureau never got emptied, Michael," said Kells. "I'll find something for you to wear. Come on, men." He tickled Nathaniel under the chin and motioned to Michael. "Let's dress for church."

Kells had never gone to church until he married Mom. He had never expressed an opinion on church. It occurred to Lily that she had no idea what Kells thought about anything.

"Poor Dennis," said Mom to Lily. "Your poor father must be heartbroken. I should call him and make sure he's all right."

Who cared if that snake was all right? What was the matter with Mom? Dennis was the creep she'd divorced, and as it turned out, for excellent reasons. Mom was a fine judge of character. "I think you should leave it alone for a while," said Lily. "Let it sort itself out. Why don't we go to the mall this afternoon while Nathaniel is napping and grab Michael a few outfits to tide him over?"

There was nothing Mom liked more than the mall. She grabbed a pencil to make a shopping list and then dropped the pencil to crush Lily in a hug. "I haven't even thanked you yet, Lily. You were so mature—getting to LaGuardia and managing Nate at the same time. I feel terrible you had to do it alone. But you rose to the occasion. I'm so proud."

Socks, she wrote at the top of her list.

Mom loved those ten-packs of socks. She felt that if you had fresh clean bright white socks on, all would be well.

But she was wrong. Socks weren't going to help. I have to tell her what really happened, thought Lily. She's the mom. She needs to know.

But she could not bring herself to damage her mother's happiness. Her son had chosen her and he needed socks. What else was there?

Lily went upstairs to fix her hair.

In the boys' room, Kells was laying out two sets of clothing. "Michael," he said, "I think Jamie might press you for details. Sometimes it's good to plan ahead how you're going to answer difficult questions. Shall we think of a line you can use when Jamie asks how come you're home?"

Jamie—who believed in perfect fathers—was in Michael's Sunday school class. And the person who remembered was the stepfather. And the person who was skeptical that Michael had gotten homesick was also the stepfather.

Lily thought, I will not cry.

"The best line," said Kells, "would be boring and easy to repeat. That way your own words don't upset you. And then change the subject. For example, 'Mom couldn't stand to have me far away, so I'm back. Tell me about third grade, Jamie. What have I missed?'"

During the second verse of the second hymn, the children left the church and went to Sunday school. When she was little, Lily had always been so eager for that second verse to come and never understood why they couldn't leave on the first verse. What was the point of waiting? So she knew why Jamie leaped off his pew, looked in disgust at Michael—who hardly seemed alive, let alone aware of what verse they were on—and jerked the bottom of Michael's tie. "Come on!" said Jamie. "What are you waiting for?" A month ago, Michael would have pummeled Jamie into little pieces for yanking him around, but this Sunday, he did not notice.

Morning sun poured through stained-glass lilies and roses. The church was hot. The velvet pew cushions were comfy. People looked sleepy.

Dr. Bordon read the text. Luke 11:5–13. The numbers sounded familiar, as if some distant Sunday school teacher had hoped Lily would memorize this.

"Jesus is speaking," Dr. Bordon said. "And he says to a crowd listening to him, 'If you had a friend, would you ever go to that friend at *midnight* and say to him, I need three loaves of bread, for another friend of mine has just arrived, and I have nothing to feed him?'"

Lily didn't know the story after all. Jesus was apt to be brief, and you'd better be paying attention or it would be over with and you wouldn't know what it meant. Half the time you wouldn't know what it meant when you *did* pay attention. Reb used to say the real miracle was that anybody figured out how to be a Christian to start with.

"'Your friend inside his house might answer you by saying, Trouble me not! My door is shut—my children are in bed. I cannot get up and give you anything.'"

Lily usually thought of church as entire, separate. A place she liked, but did not carry around with her in the same way, for example, she carried basic math into a restaurant, to figure the tip. Jesus was a remote dusty person in sandals, saying things that ended up on Sunday school walls, along with pictures of happy peasants in Sudan or India, whose lives were improved by a water buffalo donated by Sunday school children.

But this was different. This applied.

For Michael had called upon Dad for bread—meaning love; meaning home. And just like the verse, Dad had answered, "Trouble me not, Michael. I cannot get up and give you anything. My door is shut." Lily shivered with the accuracy of it.

"'I, Jesus, say to you,'" read Dr. Bordon, "'though your friend will not get up and give you what you need—*because* he is your friend, he *will* get up, and give you everything you need. And I say to you, Ask and it shall be given. Seek and you will find. Knock and the door will be opened to you. For everyone who asks—receives. Everyone who seeks—finds. To everyone who knocks—that door will open.'"

Wait a second here, thought Lily. Michael was seeking—and got slapped. Michael knocked—and had the door slammed in his face. And Michael wasn't just *asking.* He was *begging.*

Dr. Bordon continued to read. "'If a son asks his father for bread, will the father give his son a stone?'"

Yes, thought Lily. He will.

"'If the son asks for dinner, will the father put a snake in front of him? If the son asks for eggs, will the father offer a scorpion?'"

Yes. Dennis Rosetti: Scorpion Man.

"'If you, being a bad person, know that you must give good gifts to your children, think how much more your Heavenly Father will give to those who ask Him for gifts.'"

Lily could have torn a hymnbook in half. What are you up to here, Jesus? My father *did* give his son a stone. He'd do it again. He *likes* stones. Gives nothing but stones.

Turning the Sunday bulletin to the back page, she busied herself reading announcements, hoping to block out Dr. Bordon and his nonsense. The last Sunday in September, nobody had signed up to do coffee hour. Every week in October the nursery school needed volunteers. The choir was looking for tenors.

Yesterday, Lily informed God, there was fear in my brother's voice. He was not afraid of the airport. He was afraid of his father. This father you're so sure wouldn't give him a stone.

Yesterday, even an eight-year-old didn't have a friend at midnight. Listen to me, God. Asking doesn't get you what you want. Knocking on doors doesn't open them. And fathers do so give their son a stone when they ask for bread.

You're no more a father than my real father. I'm done with you, too.

* * *

Amanda did not let Lily down. She listened to the whole story, punctuating Lily's recital with cries of agony and little shouts of "Kill him!"

They were lying on towels at the edge of Amanda's pool. They had swum back and forth for fifteen minutes, which was nothing for Amanda but more than Lily usually did in a month. Lily had that nice trim feeling that comes from lots of exercise, and as usual she was convinced that from now on she would swim, swim, swim—and as usual she knew perfectly well this was not going to happen.

Amanda shivered. "I don't want to believe that your dad really did that. I bet he really came back to the airport. I bet he couldn't actually drive away. He tried to find Michael."

"No. Because if he had tried, and he didn't find Michael, he'd have called airport security." Lily pictured her father driving away. Paying highway tolls. Stopping for takeout. Unlocking an empty apartment. Watching television. Staying up for the eleven o'clock news. Worrying about the situation in the Middle East.

Not worrying about Michael.

"I bet your father is suffering," said Amanda. "Think of him, hundreds of miles from here, all day, all night, picturing his little boy alone and scared."

Lily took off her sunglasses and stared at Amanda.

"Right," said Amanda. "If he cared, he wouldn't have left his little boy alone and scared to start with. How come your mom and Kells haven't gotten to the bottom of this?"

"They're e-mailing. Thank you, Dennis, for agreeing to ship Michael's stuff. Best—Judith."

"So she didn't ask your father what happened and your father didn't say. Did Michael tell you?"

"I don't think anything happened. I think Michael was just more effort than Dad felt like. You know little boys. Michael needed laundry and breakfast and dinner and help with his reading and chauffeuring and games and attention and conversation and snacks. And he said to me on the plane, he said—oh, Amanda!—he said, *I thought we would play catch.*"

"Poor Michael. How's he doing?"

"He sort of isn't doing. Just sitting there." Lily felt strangely heavy, hanging on to everything that hurt Michael. No wonder Michael is just sitting there, she thought. He's weighted down.

Amanda slathered sunscreen on her legs and arms. "Still, Lily. Just because Dennis Rosetti is totally worthless, I'm not sure it means that God is. Let's not say it out loud. God might strike us down."

"If God planned to strike anybody," said Lily, "and if there's any justice in this world, He'd strike Dad. But no, Dad is fine."

"Well, you're right," said Amanda. "That is not fair." She smacked the sunscreen bottle down on the tiles. She got on her knees. Then she tilted her head back and glared straight up into the sky.

"What are you doing?"

"I'm praying. I'm watching closely so God can't wiggle to the side and pretend He doesn't see me. God!" she yelled. Slippery with sunscreen, ponytail wet and tight, sunglasses sliding around, long thin arms sticking straight up like a gymnast about to break her back, she pointed accusingly upward. "God! Give us revenge! I suggest a slick spot on the road. Dennis Rosetti driving too fast and braking too late! A man who abandons his third grader at the airport, God, deserves to suffer and suffer and suffer and suffer! Or die. You choose."

Amanda lay back down on her towel.

"Amen," said Lily Rosetti.

chapter

7

Who could have guessed that hate would be so fierce, so alive?

Lily had thought of "hate" as a verb for clothing (I hate pink) or school (I hate essays) or weather (I hate when it's this hot). What a misuse of the word. Hate was a burning wilderness. It occupied her like an army.

And the thing she could not get over was that Dennis Rosetti had no hate because he had no interest. His interest in Michael wasn't even enough for short-term parking.

Her Amen to Amanda's prayer pounded like a snare drum in her ears and made it impossible to think. School, which had always been friendly and bland, was a carnivore, chewing on her. And for the first semester in their lives, Lily and Amanda had no classes together and did not see each other during the day. It was like walking without a floor.

If this was life, Lily was staying home to watch television for the next fifty years.

She was thinner. She knew it was because her pulse wouldn't stop racing.

Only in church did her heart slow down. The next Sunday, for his sermon, Dr. Bordon discussed a sentence Jesus had spoken. *I will not leave you comfortless.* In the original Greek, explained Dr. Bordon, "comfortless" was literally "orphaned."

It was true. Michael was comfortless and might just as well be orphaned. A sister wasn't enough. A mother wasn't enough. A stepfather was meaningless. Michael Rosetti had no father.

Dr. Bordon implied that Jesus could fill the void. Lily thought probably you had to be a grown-up for that to work. No amount of church would comfort an eight-year-old for the loss of his father.

In the course of the week, Michael had become, in military terms, a noncombatant: a person who didn't—wouldn't—couldn't fight. All he was, was there. He didn't fail in school. In fact, because he sat still instead of yelling and running and arguing and getting into trouble, he did quite well. Teachers liked him more. After all, half the boys in school were given Ritalin to calm them down, so teachers were trained to believe that a semicomatose boy was a good boy.

Lily could hardly stand to look at her brother. He seemed middle-aged to her, as if any moment he would chair a committee or open a checking account.

Lily raced home from school every day to intercept the mail. If Mom got home first, Lily had to follow her trail, because Mom started opening mail in the front hall and continued as she moved, chucking junk mail or ripped envelopes in any wastebasket or on any surface, dropping letters on any table, setting bills near any telephone, taping anything that caught her eye to the refrigerator.

Day after day, the bill didn't come.

After school, Michael didn't get on his bike anymore and ride over to Jamie's. He didn't start projects in the cellar or hide things in the attic. He didn't talk about school and he didn't listen when Lily and Mom did.

On Wednesday of the second week, Mom and Nathaniel were in the kitchen arguing over snacks when Lily got home, and Michael was sitting at the table not taking sides.

"I wanna duice box," Nathaniel shouted. "I wanna sfig noonans."

"Lily, darling, I have to practice," said Mom, meaning, "You handle snacks." She zoomed down into the cellar, where she practiced her trumpet. Kells had put foam tiles and insulation into the cellar ceiling to absorb the sound, but if you stood over where Mom was playing, your feet vibrated.

When Nathaniel was born, Mom used to pop him into a baby backpack and take him down to the cellar with her, which was supposed to imbue his little baby heart with a love of music. Nathaniel now covered his ears whenever he saw a brass instrument.

Lily gave Nathaniel a four-pack of Fig Newtons.

"I wike sfig noonans," Nathaniel informed them. His little fingers struggled with the cellophane wrapper. "Opennuh cookie, Wiwwy."

She opened the pack for him and threw the plastic into the garbage. There lay the credit card bill, unopened.

"Frow it onna foor," Nathaniel told Lily.

"Don't throw it on the floor! Eat it!"

"No. It's onna foor now."

"It's on the floor because you threw it there. Don't throw

anything else on the floor. I can't stand it when my shoes stick."

"Foos stick," said Nate happily. "Foos stick foos stick foos stick!"

A normal Michael would have licked it up off the floor. A normal Michael would have shrieked "Foos stick" for the next half hour too. This Michael wasn't listening.

Lily could not retrieve the bill while the boys were there. Searching through the garbage for interesting envelopes was not a habit she wanted Nathaniel to develop. "Michael, start Nate's new video for him, okay?"

The new video was a particularly sappy Clifford. It was one of the million things that had made Michael want to live someplace else. A normal Michael would have taken Nathaniel outside to experiment with throwing stuff down storm drains, leaping off the carport roof or rolling each other around the yard inside the trash barrels.

This Michael sighed, nodded and followed Nate over to the television, as if the toddler were the one in charge.

Lily fished out the envelope, wiped it clean with a paper towel and stuffed it into her jeans pocket. Then she turned on the kitchen computer to see what e-mails had arrived.

Reb e-mailed like a person planning to publish a ten-volume diary. The very first afternoon at college she had met a great great great guy named Freddie. Within hours, Reb knew Freddie was perfect. In days, she and Freddie were a perfect couple. Lily knew more about Freddie than she did about the President.

This time a word popped out at her. In the header listing other addresses to whom Reb was sending the same message (her three best friends from high school, her favorite high school teacher, a cousin, Mom, Lily) Lily saw the address "denrose."

She was stunned. The snake knew the very same details about Reb's life that Lily did. But then she read the latest installment of her sister's perfect life with the perfect guy on the perfect campus with the perfect roommates and the perfect professors and she was filled with an unexpected joy.

Her sister was not comfortless. Had not been orphaned. Didn't even know that Michael and Lily had lost a parent. In fact, swept up in the wonderful new world of college, Reb seemed not to remember that Michael and Lily might also have a life. She didn't write, "How's third grade, Michael?" She didn't write, "How awful not to have Amanda in any classes!"

But that was fine. Somehow, by only an hour or two, Reb had missed the nightmare of Michael's return.

Denrose.

It sounded like a street in a new subdivision, where the builder used his children's names, so you had to live on Linda Lane or Kevin Court.

That night Lily sat up late, not doing homework. How could she pay off the credit card bill? She didn't have a checking account. Banks would know how, but Lily hated asking anybody anywhere how to do anything. She liked knowing already.

It was past eleven o'clock. Michael and Nathaniel had been asleep for ages.

The house was very quiet.

Lily heard Mom turn off the news downstairs. She heard Kells say, "Wait a minute, Judith. I wanted to see—"

"I have to talk to you about something," said Mom, and gently and completely she shut the TV room door.

It had to be about Michael. It was about time Mom started worrying about Michael. Feather light, Lily zipped down the carpeted stairs to listen in.

"He e-mailed me at school," said her mother.

There could be only one "he." Denrose. Lily had never thought of denrose reaching Mom at school. Dad could reach Mom, and Lily would never know.

"Dennis is not going to pay any more child support. He says the children don't love him and he's out of the equation."

Lily stared into the wallpaper. A picture had once hung there. She could see its little nail hole, hidden in a flower. Other people repainted and redecorated. But Mom did not see things. She only heard them. Her world was full of notes and chords and melodies.

Dad's abandoning me, too? thought Lily. He's driving away from me, too? Michael and I are out of his equation.

She had yelled—You're not my father!

Now he was yelling back—And you're not my daughter! So there!

Lily heard the distinct thud of the recliner.

Kells's favorite possession was the dusty blue corduroy recliner on which he lay to watch TV. It had a long stick handle. He'd come home from work, throw the stick and sigh with relief when he was lying there all pillowy on his back. Then he'd get a good grip on the remote and investigate every channel.

"Oh," said Kells, presumably from his recliner.

"We have to get a lawyer," said Mom. "We have to fight."

Lily had a vision of Michael, small and thin at the edge of a courtroom; of Dennis Rosetti telling a judge, He's not worth anything to me.

It wouldn't be a fight, thought Lily. It would be an execution. It would kill Michael.

"It's just money, Judith," said Kells. "Why don't we forget about it? You and I earn enough. Why even let the children know what Dennis said? Michael's back because he loves you and that's all the support you need."

But this was untrue.

Michael was not back because he loved Mom. He was back because Dad did not love him.

Mom was a whirlwind occupying some narrow music-filled space. A few minutes each day, the tornado that was Mom came to a stop. She flung herself around her children and fixed dinner and began spinning again, and you could not put your hand in her life any more than you could put your hand into the blades of a fan.

What if Mom understood that Michael had been forced to come home? Would her whirlwind stop? Would she be a fan whose motor had burned out?

"Next Saturday," said Kells, "I thought I'd take Michael to a ball game."

I'm paying airfare, thought Lily. Kells is paying time. And Dad—he's paying nothing whatsoever.

She was having a nightmare every few nights.

The dreams were full of wounded phones and angry people in uniform and passengers flinging luggage who would scream, Michael's dead, he's gone, you lost him, it's your fault.

It was never Dad's fault.

If anything happened to Michael, it was always Lily's fault.

Tonight, the police in the nightmare took Michael away for stealing the teddy bear, while Lily ran screaming alongside the police car, dragging Nathaniel by his pitching arm, bumping him against cement lane dividers until eventually he fell apart and she had only his arm.

It was a more vivid dream than usual.

When she woke up, it was sticking to her, like the phone, crawling on her skin.

Lily got up, stumbling blindly to the bathroom. She filled an old-fashioned red rubber hot-water bottle and took it back to bed with her.

What kind of nightmares did Michael have?

Michael was astonished when Kells told him about the baseball plan. His stepfather loved sports, but only watching them on TV while lying in his recliner. Real-life sports were way out past Kells's energy level.

But as family trips went, this was a big improvement over the usual September stuff. Mom liked to drive north on the Taconic Parkway and Look at Leaves. Her other September trip was: Winter Coats—Do They Fit? Or: Mittens—Do We Need More?

Since Michael had never pulled an actual mitten over his actual fingers, but zipped them up for the winter in a jacket pocket, the Mitten trip was lost on him.

And here was Kells, offering minor-league baseball.

Michael would certainly rather have gone to see the Yankees. But baseball was baseball.

Nobody else went. Not Mom, not Lily, not even Nathaniel. Michael worried for a few miles of the drive that Kells wanted to talk. But he didn't.

They sat six rows above the visiting team's dugout. Michael had not known there would be a sing-along, with the words on a huge digital board at the back of the field. He had not dreamed that the entire crowd would sing "Take Me Out to the Ball Game."

I'm at the ball game with the wrong father, thought Michael.

* * *

Lily spent Saturday at Amanda's. Amanda was an only child who led a leisurely life. She was always stretched out on something: a chaise by the pool, a sofa by the fire, a couch by the TV. And she did this in cleanliness and neatness, because a housekeeper did every chore that got skipped at Lily's house.

Lily told Amanda about the late-night conversation.

"When's the court date?" asked Amanda.

"There isn't one. Kells says he can take care of us and why should Mom get all worked up and lose sleep and hire lawyers when all it is, is money."

"Kells isn't so bad," said Amanda, referring to hundreds of conversations in which Lily and Reb and Michael had wanted Kells to dry up and blow away. "But you've got to tell Kells and your mother what happened and they've got to go after the money. Your father has to pay. Denrose gets to abandon Michael, terrify Michael, humiliate and crush Michael—and then get off free?"

"Pretty much."

"I wonder how he'll spend all that nice money he's saving by not paying child support."

Lily knew instantly that denrose was buying a car. Something fabulous and expensive and beyond his means. But not beyond his means now.

She saw him tenderly parking his new car crosswise at

the far end of parking lots, so it wouldn't get dinged. Because the finish on your car matters more than the heart of your son.

* * *

They were at the bottom of the third.

"Kells?" asked Michael.

"Yup."

"May I have a snack?"

"Sure." Kells handed him a ten-dollar bill.

Michael waited to hear the rules—it has to be nutritious; it can't be fried; be back in exactly five minutes—but Kells said nothing.

"You want something too?" asked Michael.

"Not yet."

"I can go by myself?"

"Sure."

Mom would never have allowed it. But the stadium was small and fully enclosed and packed with parents and officials. They both knew he was fine. Michael climbed the steps toward the shaded upper tier of the stadium, where the concessions were. He surveyed each concession to decide exactly what he wanted. He passed ice cream and considered popcorn. He was approaching pretzels and tacos when he saw his father—his father!—lifting a gray cardboard tray of soft drinks from a counter.

Michael sprinted down the polished cement. There were as many obstacles in his path as there had been at the airport. Kids and parents and strollers and trash cans and vendors of autographed programs. He weaved desperately among them.

Dad balanced the tray of soft drinks with one hand and

dropped change in his pocket with the other, and then he moved through an ice cream line and out of sight.

Red T-shirt, Michael told himself. Jeans. No socks. Just like always.

He flung himself through the ice cream line. Fifty feet ahead of him, the red T-shirt and jeans were ambling along and Michael tore after him. "Dad!" he shouted.

His father did not turn.

"Dad!" He caught up before he expected to, and they collided. The tray of sodas crashed to the ground and the plastic lids snapped off and soda spilled everywhere.

The man was a complete stranger.

"I'm sorry," Michael whispered. "I thought you were—umm—my dad." He was afraid of crying. He had promised himself he would never cry again. Not in this life. Not for anything. "Here's—umm—my snack money. Because I—umm—wrecked your sodas."

The man who wasn't his father squatted down, bouncing a little on his heels, so now he was beneath Michael instead of above him. "Where is your dad?" said the man gently.

"Washington," whispered Michael.

And the stranger nodded, as if he knew a thing or two about fathers who were in Washington. "It's okay," he said to Michael. "It was an accident."

Michael managed to back away and find the right set of stairs and get down them without falling. He slid over people's knees and collapsed into his seat. He knew the man was watching. He knew he should glance back and wave or something.

He sat as small and motionless as he could.

He could not quite see the game or hear the announcer.

After a long time, Michael put the ten-dollar bill back in Kells's hand.

chapter

8

Every seven days, Lily was forced to sit in church and consider the role of God. God, however, took just as much interest in her and in Michael as their real father did: zero.

God understood what was going on just as much as their mother did: zero.

Zero plus zero equals zero.

Nice equation, God, Lily told Him.

Dr. Bordon read the morning's scripture. Matthew 18:21.

It was about Peter. Lily was drawn to Peter, a follower of Jesus who was often puzzled. This time Peter wanted to know how often he had to forgive somebody who had sinned against him. Seven times? Peter asked hopefully.

Lily too kept count. She imagined this brawny fisherman with his big strong fingers spread out, ticking off previous forgivenesses, because surely the other guy's forgiveness allotment was used up. The guy was out there hoping for Forgiveness Number Eight—and there wasn't one! This afternoon, Peter could smash him in the face.

And Jesus—annoying as always—answered, You have to forgive seventy times seven.

Lily took the little pew pencil—for filling out a card if you wanted a visit from the minister, which numbered down there with the last thing on earth Lily would ever want—and wrote out the arithmetic. Seventy times seven equaled four hundred ninety.

What kind of answer is that? Peter probably muttered.

It always surprised Lily that none of the disciples ever said, I'm out of here. I liked being a fisherman better.

Lily was fond of word problems, the kind that began, "If Madison drives twenty-six miles at sixty-five miles an hour, while Emmett . . ." Now she made up her own forgiveness arithmetic word problem. If Dad had Michael for eighteen days, and Dad was mean and rotten twenty times each of those days . . . No good. That was only three hundred sixty. Three hundred sixty from four hundred ninety meant Dad could get a hundred thirty more forgivenesses.

Okay, fine. If Dad had been rotten to Michael *thirty* times a day, which was perfectly possible, then he was over his quota. Lily didn't have to waste time forgiving denrose anything.

A hand slid over her shoulder and plucked the pew paper from her grip. For a fraction of a second, Lily thought it was Jesus, truly provoked. She whipped around.

The hand belonged to Trey Mahanna, older brother of Jamie.

Jamie's family really was perfect. The dad was perfect, and so was the mom. The four grandparents, all of whom Lily knew, were perfect. The older sisters, prettily named Ashley and April, were perfect. The Mahanna house was perfect, and probably their vacations. Their laundry did not lie in overflowing baskets at the bottom of the stairs, and if it did, the children didn't vault over it and continue with their lives; Trey and Ashley and April probably sorted it neatly and did Jamie's for him while they were at it.

Last year, Trey had been at a low point in life, having gotten braces, pimples, glasses and a concave chest all at once.

This year, however, Trey's complexion was under control, he had contacts and he'd grown some crucial inches. Weight lifting was beginning to have a noticeable effect. He'd have the braces for a while yet, but at least he hadn't succumbed to temptation and gone with blue or orange bands. "Who?" whispered Trey, tapping her shoulder with her own stolen pew card.

Pew conversations were difficult to conduct over the shoulder, especially with everybody else silently listening to Dr. Bordon. "Who what?" murmured Lily, trying not to move her lips.

"Who has to be forgiven twenty or else thirty times eighteen?"

The pew pencil was very small, like a golf score pencil. As a weapon, it wouldn't be confiscated at an airport X-ray. But Lily could have stabbed Trey through the eye with it. *God* didn't know, *Mom* didn't know, *Reb* didn't know, *denrose* didn't know—and Trey Mahanna knew right away what was gnawing at Lily Rosetti's heart.

She hated him. She hated his stupid perfect family.

Dr. Bordon talked on placidly about forgiveness, as if forgiveness were a sweet simple event—like deciding whether to get soft ice cream or regular. Probably the biggest thing Dr. Bordon ever had to forgive in *his* family was not flossing.

Forgiveness rots, Lily said to God. Listen to me. You didn't totally let me down, because I found Michael in the end, and we did get home. Thank you. But you fell down on the job when you created Dennis Rosetti. I don't want to forgive him. I want him to pay. Don't pretend you didn't try that yourself on the people you hated. Read your own books! You know how this is done.

Make him suffer.

* * *

After church, the Rosetti/Nickerson family did not go home because it was Fall Picnic.

The church had lovely grounds, long and green under spreading maples and tulip trees. Here, the entire Sunday school played the kind of games that didn't exist anywhere except at picnics: three-legged races, rope pulls, egg-on-a-spoon relays and sack races. The food was outstanding and the choices were infinite. Last names A to M brought main dishes, while N to Z were responsible for salad or dessert. Trey's perfect mother, of course, always brought not one, but two yummy seafood casseroles following her own secret recipes, while Mom raced into a 24/7 grocery on the way to church and picked up a frozen cake.

It was the role of older kids to assist the little ones. Lily was assigned the egg race. The eggs were not hard-boiled. Some kids—like Nathaniel—loved making a gooey yellow mess, and were happier smashing their eggs than getting to the finish line, while other kids cried with anxiety over the stress, and wanted Lily to take the risk of carrying the egg on its spoon while they trotted along next to her and got the credit.

Trey, meanwhile, organized the tug-of-war between the six-year-olds and the fives. He staged the war across a huge mud puddle, because getting truly dirty was uncommon for most children; some mothers were genuinely shocked at the sight of filth on their babies. Trey made everybody take off their shoes and socks and then promised that the winning team got to shove the other team in the mud.

"Hey, Amanda!" yelled Trey. "Help me out here. My fives need strength!"

Amanda did only clean things and therefore was handling Drop the Clothespin into the Large Mason Jar and Get a Prize. Nothing would draw her into a mud situation. "Hey, Lily!" shrieked Amanda. "Trey needs you!"

Lily was on her last egg lap, so she joined the fives.

"Lily, on you I will practice my motivational skills," said Trey. He was laughing. "Think of my team as the guy who has to be forgiven twenty—or else thirty—times eighteen. Pull hard enough on this rope, and you strangle him."

With such an incentive, Lily and her fives, although outnumbered and smaller, easily whipped Trey and his sixes. Everybody thrashed joyfully in the mud while Lily and Trey slipped away before the parents figured out who was responsible. They drifted behind a bunch of adults who were pretending to be on Atkins diets or South Beach diets but were actually scarfing up seconds on cake and pie.

Trey did not want to discuss mud or desserts. "So who is it?" he said. "Your father? Can't be anyone else. Michael was going to live with his dad forever and he's back in a minute and a half? Comes over to play with Jamie and he's practically in a coma instead of being good old Michael? My father says Michael needs counseling. My father says—"

How dare Trey Mahanna analyze Michael? How dare his family talk about Michael, as if Michael were their business? How dare they notice stuff Mom had failed to notice? "Get away from me, Trey. I hate you and your whole stupid family."

* * *

At least Lily was enjoying her classes. Biology, French 1, Latin 2, European History and English. The amount of homework was appalling, but Lily loved it. She loved the shape of foreign languages and the frame of history. She loved biology and the surprises of nature. In English, they were doing plays, and she loved when her turn came and she got to read a part out loud. She especially liked being the bad guy and shouting terrible things.

Trey was in her biology class. Monday morning, when she left for school, Lily told herself miserably that she had to apologize to Trey. The Mahannas were the ones being *nice* to Michael. Michael needed Jamie. Lily couldn't go around telling the only nice family out there that she hated them.

But Trey was no longer in her biology class. He had gotten to school earlier than she had that morning—and changed his schedule. He was in a different biology section.

The power of telling somebody you hated them stunned Lily. She had done it twice in one month, and successfully removed two people from her life. If you called that success.

From biology—in which she hardly even saw the teacher, never mind opened her book to the right page—she trudged on to Latin, where the teacher passed out forms.

"We're going to keep track of you guys," she explained to her class. "You will be followed throughout your high school careers to see what effect learning Latin has on your knowledge of English. Of course I'm hoping you'll all take four years of Latin and that on your SATs you'll score very very very high due to my outstanding teaching of this riveting language. Anyway, this is the parental permission paperwork."

Lily was elated. The time had come. She could leave "Father" blank.

But the form had only one line.

PARENT OR GUARDIAN:

She couldn't even skip denrose on paper.

* * *

Once more, sitting by Amanda's pool after school, she told Amanda everything.

"Lily," said Amanda, "I still say you have to tell your mother and Kells. It's just going more sour."

"I promised Michael."

"It was a dumb promise. You knew that when you made it."

In this decade, promises were flexible. You kept a promise only if it worked out well for you. This was true if you were President or a high school teacher. Anywhere—marriage—business—government—church, if a promise got too annoying, you just broke it. Everybody knew that.

"Michael won't even talk to *you*," Amanda pointed out.

This was true. Lily and Michael had agreed not to talk to other people, but Lily had not expected to be one of them. Michael wouldn't tell Lily one thing. Now and then she brought it up. "If we told Mom . . ."

"No!" Michael would cry. "You promised." He had

seemed so young to her when he said that. So thin and little. A toddler at the playground, calling out the brief desperate judgments of little kids—That isn't fair! You promised!

Amanda came up with a dozen solid excuses why Lily should break a foolish promise to a little boy. When she sat with her best friend in the sun, it was clear: Amanda knew how to handle things. When Lily got home and saw Michael, it wasn't so clear.

* * *

Monday evenings, Mom was never home. She rehearsed the community band. She loved teaching adults for a change. The band was doing a Gustav Holst suite called *The Planets.* Mom played the CD continually, studying her full score, directing an invisible orchestra, bringing in an invisible oboe and getting more substance from invisible strings. Lily e-mailed Reb that if she had to listen to *The Planets* one more time, she would go into orbit.

Mom's musical life was so absorbing that she assumed everybody else's life was equally absorbing. Kells, on the other hand, was a tired kind of guy who didn't much like his job and had a long, difficult commute. As usual, the moment Mom left for rehearsal, Kells headed for the TV room, backed into his recliner, dropped, flipped and flattened.

The recliner used to make Reb crazy. "Kells really is a dusty blue corduroy recliner kind of a guy," she used to complain. "I'll never know why Mom married him."

The four of them were in the TV room. Kells watched baseball. Nathaniel struggled with a jigsaw that had three pieces. Michael lay on his back on the carpet, thinking ceiling thoughts. Lily was facedown on the couch, so she could moan now and then and slam her forehead against her Latin book.

Kells turned the television off.

In the sudden quiet, Nathaniel put his puzzle pieces down. Lily glanced over at her stepfather. Even Michael turned his head.

"So what really happened?" said Kells.

* * *

Michael had been lying on his back, his eyes fixed on the ceiling.

Today at the mall—there were four malls Mom loved, each (according to Mom) with a different atmosphere—Michael had spent several minutes in a card shop. Greeting cards were difficult to read, with their peculiar script and meaningless poetic thoughts. He found no card to send to his father.

Reb e-mailed Dad. Michael couldn't do that. He lost track of sentences he had to create by himself. Of course there was the telephone. But although he desperately wanted Dad to call him, he did not want to call Dad.

Mom was speeding home from the mall when Michael saw his father coming out of a convenience store with a quart of milk. His heart leaped, his eyes watered and he had to stifle a scream to his mother—Stop the car! It's Dad!—and even though Michael knew it wasn't Dad, it was Dad.

Mom turned a corner and the man was no longer in sight. The minute she parked, Michael told his mother he was going over to Jamie's, and his mother of course believed him, because she was that sort of person, very believing, which you would think somebody teaching high school would have gotten over by now. Michael sped back to the convenience store, even though he knew he couldn't get there in time and the man wasn't his father anyway.

Kells wants to know what happened, thought Michael dully. He turned his face to the ceiling again. He didn't know. Except he hadn't been good enough.

"Happened?" said his sister in a casual voice.

"About Michael coming home," said their stepfather. "I need to know."

Nathaniel beamed at his father. "Inna pane," he explained.

"Right," said Kells. "You and Lily went to pick up Michael from the plane."

"No," said Nathaniel, irritated. *"I went inna pane!"*

It was an impressive sentence for a little boy not two years old: correcting his very own daddy; explaining his big adventure; telling the truth.

Michael did not back him up. Neither did Lily.

Kells sighed. After a while he said, "How about popcorn?"

"Popcorn!" shouted Nathaniel, who found the hot-air popper mesmerizing. He raced back and forth from the kitchen keeping Michael and Lily informed. "Popping!" he shouted. And on the next trip, "Butter!"

Michael looked at his sister. He knew she wanted to tell. He knew Amanda was on the telling side. "Don't," said Michael. "Don't talk about anything." Michael had not figured out how to repair things, but he could keep it from getting worse. Silence was his only choice.

"Kells isn't so bad, Michael," said his sister softly.

Kells was now taking him somewhere every Saturday, and Jamie's dad, Mr. Mahanna, was taking him somewhere every Sunday afternoon. Lily was right. It wasn't so bad. But good—that was something else.

Nathaniel dropped a stack of paper napkins all over Michael. "Keep kween!" he shouted.

"Who wants to keep clean eating popcorn?" said Lily. "Half the fun is spreading the butter around."

Kells came back with the popcorn. He had poured it into a heavy white bowl with a wide blue stripe. He flopped into the recliner and held it on his lap, so he could have some control over the mess. If they wanted popcorn they were going to have to crawl for it. He found the remote and clicked the ball game back on. As was often the case with baseball, nothing had happened.

Nathaniel climbed into his daddy's lap, arranging himself around the bowl and completely blocking Kells's view of the television.

Lily flailed an arm in the air, but no popcorn arrived, so she rolled off the couch and crawled across the carpet, taking a route over Michael's body and digging her kneecaps into his ribs so he'd have to do *something.* At least scream in agony. But he didn't.

She felt as if she could see through him; as if he were not a person anymore, but liquid; a pool of water. All that was left was his reflection.

She had some popcorn, finding out once again that butter and salt are as good as it gets, and crawled back to the sofa.

"Come on, guys," said Kells. "What happened, Lily? Tell me about it."

"I know what," said Michael. "Nathaniel, you feed me. Throw the popcorn into my mouth, Nate."

Nathaniel favored his brother with a huge smile, and began hurling popcorn everywhere. Not one kernel came close. Michael got onto his knees and opened his mouth wide to be a better target. Lily took the pottery bowl and knelt between Nate and Michael, supplying ammunition and assisting Nate's throwing hand, and still Nate did not manage to get anything in Michael's mouth, and they were all laughing—real laughter, happy laughter—the first Lily had heard from Michael since before the visit to denrose— and Kells said, "You see, Michael, a few weeks ago, we got an e-mail."

Lily had been about to tell the truth, because Amanda was right and Kells was right; the parents had to know.

But Kells was headed in a whole different direction.

Michael did not know about the e-mail. Michael did not know his real father was not going to send one more dollar to pay the cost of Michael's life on earth. Michael did not know that not only had he been thrown out of his father's house, not only had he been thrown out of his father's car, but he was also thrown out of his father's checkbook.

"There's the question of child—" Kells went on.

Oh, Kells, I hate you, too! thought Lily. How dare you tell Michael that denrose is gleefully no longer paying child support?

God is lying. There are no friends at midnight.

Lily flung the heavy bowl into the television and smashed the screen.

* * *

The school psychologist's tiny waiting room had one tiny window, tightly curtained. It had four old wooden chairs, painted yellow. It had one poster of cheerful meerkats and one of a whale whose expression was unreadable. Its interior door was tightly closed so nobody could see into or hear anything from the actual office where the actual counseling happened.

Or, in Lily's case, didn't happen.

Lily had asked herself a hundred times whether to tell Mom and Kells, but she hadn't asked herself once whether to tell a school shrink. Never. Still, hiding her rage for thirty solid minutes made second-year Latin look easy.

Hate is un-American. Americans are supposed to like everybody; supposed to make excuses for everybody. "Aw, give him a second chance," you're supposed to say, whether he's a mass murderer or a high school vandal.

"Aw, she didn't mean to," you insist, whether she's a shoplifter of lipsticks or a corporate thief of millions.

"Aw, he couldn't help it," you point out, whether he's a hit-and-run driver or a cheater in arithmetic.

But Dennis Rosetti had had chances. He *had* meant to. He *could* have helped it.

The outer hall door opened. Lily looked out to see who her fellow sufferer was and it was Trey Mahanna. They stared at each other. "*You're* in counseling?" she said.

"*Me?*" Trey was appalled that she could think such a thing. "Of course not. I just bumped into Dr. Sherman down the hall and he asked me to tell his next patient that he'll be another five minutes and for you not to leave."

I'm the *patient*? thought Lily.

"What are you in for?" asked Trey, cheerful as a meerkat.

"Anger management."

Trey laughed. "I should have guessed."

"Get out of here, Trey."

"Lemme give you some advice," said Trey. "The key to ending this torture is to let Dr. Sherman talk. You don't have to listen or anything. Nobody else does. Then, at the end of the session, you go, 'Oh. I see. *Thank* you.' Then he's all happy because he illuminated your otherwise dark and pointless existence." Trey laughed again. "You plan to tell Dr. Sherman about the twenty or thirty times eighteen?"

How dare Trey give her advice? How dare he mention the seventy times seven? Nothing in her entire existence had ever been so important, so personal or so terrible. It was a trespass, and Trey was a trespasser in the sense of the Lord's Prayer—*those who trespass against us*.

There were no weapons in the room other than the chairs. Lily grabbed the heavy wooden back of one chair and hoisted it over her head.

The school psychologist opened the door.

Under his shocked stare, Lily set the chair back down. Carefully. She was going to be in Anger Management for years.

"We were flirting," said Trey, his expression as unreadable as the whale's. "Cavewoman style."

chapter
9

Reb didn't come home from college until Thanksgiving. She was stunned and offended to find a completely different family. "Who are you guys, anyway?" Reb demanded of Michael and Lily. "I don't even know you!"

Perhaps she had assumed that her family would stay exactly the same. She would dip into Lily and Michael and Mom and Kells and Nathaniel, as one dipped a toe into water at the pool, and they would be the same temperature, color and depth they had been before. But the force of a single day had changed Lily the way September 11 and the destruction of the World Trade Center had changed America. Some parts of Lily were no longer standing. Some parts of her were stronger. Michael—who was Michael after that?

Lily never knew. The busy, talky, dirty, exuberant little boy who left in August came back in body only. The kid who used to ride his bike off the shed roof and use his safety helmet for a kickball was gone.

At dinner Wednesday night of Thanksgiving break, Reb asked things like—"How's your divorce support group, Mom?" an activity they had all forgotten about. It seemed a hundred years ago. Reb didn't ask Kells anything. He was just so much furniture to her. And quickly, she lost interest in what other people might be doing, and shifted into talking about herself, her friends, her classes, her fun times and her wonderful wonderful perfect boyfriend, Freddie.

Reb had catapulted into a new world so demanding and rewarding and full of love that she barely remembered the existence of earlier worlds. Reb had gotten what Michael had hoped for. Perhaps it was too much to ask that out of one small family, two children could have their dreams come true.

The more Reb chattered, the more exhausted Mom and Kells and Michael and even Nathaniel became by her presence. But Lily had the odd sensation of falling in love with her sister. There was something enchanting about a person so sure that she had the best life on earth.

The joy of reunion lasted until nine-fifteen that evening, when the twenty-three-month-old in their midst was way past his bedtime. Since the evening Michael had come home and given him sleeping orders, Nathaniel had gone to bed easily. But the excitement of his big sister being here was too much. Although his eyes were red from rubbing, his mouth drooping, his shoulders sagging, Nate screamed and fought being taken to bed. Hauled bodily up the stairs, he gripped the railings and kicked the walls, refusing to lie down in his crib. When he got left there anyway, it was motivating; in two seconds he learned how to climb out. Mom and Kells grimly carried him back up again, and twice more he came stumbling and sobbing down the stairs. Reb said to Michael, "I thought *I* had a tough room-mate. You must hate him."

"He's okay," said Michael, which was immediately proved wrong as Nathaniel moved into full tantrum mode. Reb watched incredulously, as if she had known people were stupid enough to have kids, but hadn't known she would be expected to tolerate one.

"I'll take him up this time," said Michael. "I'll sleep with him."

"No!" said Reb. "Mother! Ruining Michael's life is not the solution to a spoiled brat. Discipline Nathaniel for a change!"

Mom did not look glad to have Reb home.

"He's just tired," said Michael, taking his little brother.

Upstairs, Michael squinched himself into the crib with Nathaniel and put his arm around his little brother's back, both for comfort and to force him down. "Go to sleep now, Nate. I'm staying."

In spite of the night-light, Michael had a dark moment, the dark of his first night in the new house, when York got torn from his arms, when the door got closed, when his father's last words were "Grow up!" and Michael was alone in the dark.

"I'm staying," said Michael again.

"Okie, Mikoo," mumbled Nathaniel, and he slept, limp on his wrinkled sheets, and Michael felt a sort of terror for him.

Thanksgiving Day was very busy. Mom's family came, Kells's family came, even Dad's family came, because of course they still loved Reb and Lily and Michael, and they were hanging on wherever they could. Mom roasted the turkey, because even she could shove a bird in the oven and take it out again later. The relatives arrived with enough dishes and desserts to feed another church picnic. All the grown-ups were careful and polite and accommodating so that mention of divorce did not raise its ugly head.

Most of the talking was done by Reb, correcting each relative and making them call her Rebecca now.

All the whining was done by Nathaniel.

When the Rosetti children were in the kitchen scraping dishes to go in the dishwasher, and Nathaniel was with his grandparents in the living room, hideously overdue for a nap, Reb said, "Michael, you have got to tell Mom you want my bedroom so you can be by yourself. Nate is too awful to bother with. I don't plan to come home a lot anyway after this. You might as well have your own room."

Michael was horrified that Reb didn't plan to come home a lot. He wanted to deliver a response that would please Reb, so that she'd change her mind and come home a lot after all, but he had not figured out how to please Dad and he could not marshal a plan to please Reb, either. He only knew he would never ask Mom to give him Reb's room.

Because for Nathaniel at least, Michael was joy.

* * *

Lily hadn't been able to sleep off her rage against Dad. She couldn't shop it off or run it off, eat it off or party it off. She hadn't even been able to smash it with a bowl. But she knew she and her sister would stay up all night, and at last, to Reb, Lily could confide everything. Reb would understand and care and give advice and make everything better. If she could just tell Reb, and have Reb cry with her, she wouldn't be so angry.

And God. Lily wanted to talk about God.

Lily had tried to get rid of God. She told God she hated Him, didn't believe in Him, wasn't listening to Him again. But she could not crawl out from under religion. She turned her back—there it was on the other side. She slammed the door—there it was in the next room. She closed her mind— there it was in her heart.

"Reb," she began.

"Shut the door tight," said Reb. "I'm totally exhausted from Kells's relatives. You forget when you get a stepparent that you have to tolerate yet more grandparents. I don't like them much. And Nathaniel! Listen, Lily, come visit me. You need a rest from Little Prince Whiny. You're so smart, you can skip a few days of school. You'll love it at my college. You'll love Freddie. Actually, you'll love not being *here*. And what's the matter with Michael? He used to have a personality. Take a train up to Rochester or make Kells buy you a plane ticket. He might as well be good for something."

Lily flinched. Reb didn't notice. "Kells isn't so bad," said Lily finally.

"Let's set a date. How about the second weekend in December?"

"But doesn't Christmas break start about then? Won't you be headed home only a few days after that?"

"No. Don't tell Mom, but I'm spending Christmas break

with Freddie. Four whole weeks. I was going to split my vacation between here and there, but I've changed my mind. I forgot how messy Mom is. It's like living in a Laundromat. Plus Nathaniel! Ugh. And I can't wait to see Texas. Did I tell you about Freddie's house there?"

Twice, thought Lily. But she said, "No. Tell me about Freddie's house."

Sunday morning when they went to church, Michael was amazed to find that it was no longer Thanksgiving. It was the first Sunday in Advent. It was still November, yet here they were, skidding into Christmas.

In Sunday school, Michael's teacher discussed the Star of Christmas. Had it actually been a comet? Maybe the juxtaposition of two planets? Had there been a star at all? Probably the whole thing was a myth, giving simple peasants something sparkly in the midst of their dreary lives.

Only a minute ago, Michael had believed in Santa. He did not want to hear that the Christmas star was just another con game. He decided his Sunday school teacher was a loser (there was evidence of this already) and he stopped listening.

He was taking Christmas seriously, the way it needed to be taken.

Dad didn't remember my birthday in October, thought Michael, but that's okay. He was busy and he's still mad. He forgot that I would be nine years old. But nobody doesn't remember Christmas. He'll remember Christmas.

Michael thought about UPS.

FedEx.

The post office.

That company wonderfully named G.O.D.—Guaranteed Overnight Delivery.

He hoped the presents from Dad would be delivered by G.O.D. Dad would write a Christmas card too, and Christmas morning, Dad would call. Probably he'd call earlier, to make sure the box came. Everything would be all right, because that was what Christmas was, the day when everything was all right.

* * *

The following morning was Monday, and in school Michael's teacher carefully wrote the date on the board and Michael saw that it was the first of December. Wild excitement seized him.

From then on, every day the moment he got home, he would check both the front and the back steps for packages. His father's handwriting was a square linked print, and he always used black ink.

The days plunged off the edge of the calendar, throwing themselves at December 25.

On television, advertising gave Michael hope. Dad was seeing these things. He couldn't help connecting the ads to Michael.

The days diminished in which Dad still had time. Eight more shopping days! the television would scream. Seven! Six!

Once Michael wept. He was just lying there on his back, while Nathaniel slept on the other side of the divider, and then Michael's face was covered with tears and his pillow was wet. He had promised himself never ever to cry again, and here his eyes were crying without him.

On December 24, they went to the earliest Christmas Eve service, the one for really little kids who had to be in bed by eight. The only way Nathaniel was going to bed by eight was if Michael went with him. Michael had been feeling numb all day. He might as well feel numb in bed.

The chancel of the church was one big wonderful stable, filled with real animals brought from farms and backyards. There were a donkey, a goose, four rabbits, two sheep and a pony. Michael loved animals. Sometimes he wanted to be a veterinarian. He pretended that Mom wanted pets this year, even though she insisted that their lives were too chaotic and nobody was home to love and feed and walk a pet. Maybe tomorrow under the tree Michael would find a puppy and some kittens.

It suddenly came to Michael that Dad had mailed the big box of Christmas presents to *Mom*. And Mom had hidden it away with all *her* gifts! In the morning, under the tree, there would be presents wrapped with shiny paper and tied with ribbons and bows. Plastered all over them would be gift tags. In Dad's big square black linked print, each tag would say:

To Michael
With Love,
Dad

It didn't matter what was in the boxes. There didn't even have to be boxes. He just wanted the words.

Christmas Eve had a limited number of sermon topics, and since everybody actually came to sing Christmas carols and watch the children watch the animals, the sermon had to be short.

Lily had tossed religion in the trash, but Christmas Eve didn't count; it was perfect on its own. You didn't have to believe any of this stuff to be totally happy.

The donkey was making an amazing racket. Mom called it braying. Lily thought it was the sound of being strangled alive. The goose, rabbits and sheep looked on in silent astonishment while the pony ate the hay in the manger and the children's choir giggled. The Baby Jesus, who actually was a baby, waved at his real mother in the front pew. Nathaniel, who loved to wave, shouted "Jesus! Over here!" which was just how Lily felt all the time.

Dr. Bordon spoke of the inn, and how it was full, and how some hearts were too full of themselves to see that there were empty hearts all around that were in need.

Lily watched Michael. He hadn't sung the carols. He didn't see the three kings. He seemed unaware of the candles lit after the last carol, while everyone promised to hold up the Light of the World.

His heart is empty, thought Lily.

She was going to start bawling. It was a good word for the kind of sobbing she wanted to do, the way "bray" was a good word for what the donkey was doing. Lily wanted a huge raw sound to come out of her, and tears by the bucket, the kind of crying that left you with more headache but less heartache.

She too had expected love at Christmas.

But at least on Christmas morning Lily had the joy of sharing Christmas with a two-year-old. Nathaniel was thrilled by the wrapping paper and the ribbons and the great and wonderful privilege of ripping it all off. An especially fine box (containing a set of red fire engines) was just the right size to sit in while Michael pelted him with crushed wrapping paper balls. No one could coax Nathaniel to bother with the fire engines themselves so that they could take a photograph and send it to the giver.

Reb had taken up knitting at college. She had made Michael a yellow cap and mittens with his initials stitched in green. When they all telephoned Reb in Texas, Michael said, "The mittens are very lovely, Reb. Thank you for all the time it took to make them."

Michael—who previously would have used stupid old mittens as tinder for a bonfire in the snow! Lily hated how *old* Michael was this year.

When Nathaniel opened *his* mittens and cap, he was puzzled and quickly moved on to more rewarding gifts. "Say thank you," prompted Mom when it was Nathaniel's turn on the phone with Reb. But Nathaniel remained silent.

"He's a little young for the joy of hand-knits," Lily told her sister, but Reb didn't laugh.

✳ ✳ ✳

In the late afternoon, as always, friends, neighbors and relatives came by for dessert.

But the relative Michael cared about did not call.

All day long, all through dinner, all into the evening, he still believed the phone would ring. Because nobody doesn't remember Christmas.

Around eleven o'clock at night, some kids from Mom's band showed up and serenaded her with "Jingle Bells." Everybody came in for hot chocolate with marshmallows.

Michael stayed close by the phone, in case the racket of all those instruments and all that talk drowned out the ringing that mattered.

Finally Lily said to him, "It's twelve o'clock, Michael. Let's go to bed."

Twelve o'clock.

So Christmas had come. And gone.

Slowly, silently, he followed his sister up the stairs, and at the top of the stairs Lily turned right to go into her bedroom while Michael turned left to go into the room he shared with Nathaniel.

Lily went into her room.

She looked out the window at the sparkling lights on roofs and trees.

She opened the window to let chilly snow-tonight wind blow in.

Lily said to the birthday boy, "It's midnight, Jesus. And you're wrong.

"There are no friends at midnight."

part two:
the following
september

*

chapter

10

When school began again the following September, Lily had high hopes for her junior year. Age sixteen was such an improvement over age fifteen: Lily could drive her own car, earn her own money and leave the babysitting to others. Along with the pleasure of new notebooks, new pencils, new clothes and, best of all, totally excellent new shoes, was that first-day-of-school joy. A fresh new year in which to get things right for a change.

Of course, no sooner had the satisfying rhythm of class begun than they had a Teacher Work Day.

Students didn't have school, but Lily's mother had to show up at her school for Teacher Improvement, and Kells didn't have the day off, so Mom and Kells were out the door and into their cars as early as ever. Michael had been invited to go on the last all-day sail of the season with the Mahannas, while Amanda had agreed to keep Nathaniel for the hours that Lily was at work.

For Lily had a job.

Since both Reb and Lily had had four years of orthodonture, Dr. Alzina knew Lily well. The day she graduated to a nighttime-only retainer, her orthodontist said, "So, Lily, you want to work for me? Two afternoons a week and alternate Saturdays?"

Lily loved the orthodontists' office. Her first job was to answer the phone and say cheerily, "Good afternoon! Doctors Bence, Alzina and Gladwin, orthodontists. This is Lily! How may I help you?"

Her second job was to hand out free toothbrushes on the off chance that an actual living kid would voluntarily brush his or her teeth.

Her third job was taking the Polaroids of Befores and Afters.

Befores were hideous: gap-toothed, beaverish, crooked-mouthed urchins with terrified eyes.

Afters were beautiful: each smile perfect and each face wreathed in pride.

Not only did Lily get to skip the icky parts of dental offices, like saliva, she earned money. Almost a year after the terrible plane flights, she had finally earned back the airplane ticket money.

It was nice not to have to babysit Nathaniel for free. Then not only could Lily turn him over to Amanda, but also she could go earn money that, at last, she could spend on herself. Lily was working all day on Teacher Work Day, because the receptionist hadn't found a sitter and had to stay home with *her* kids. Lily strapped Nathaniel into his car seat (he was a three-car-seat kid, since he got strapped down wherever he went). She braced herself. He would now burst into song.

Nathaniel had started nursery school over the summer. He was an old hand now—he knew how to sit in a circle around the keyboard and everything. But did he learn fun little rhymes like "The Farmer in the Dell" or "In and Out the Windows"? No. He came home singing ditties like *Stay home; lock the doors; wear your safety helmet; help with chores.*

This was the most depressing list Lily had ever heard. How come they weren't teaching kids to go everywhere and do everything? All previously brave three-year-olds were going to become scaredy-cats.

How contradictory were the orders of teachers. Here in nursery school, teachers did everything they could to tamp down energy and daring. Then in high school, teachers tried to retrieve it. Be free! they cried. Find your own life. Set your own boundaries. Be spontaneous. How, Lily wanted to know, when school had so busily been destroying all those skills since age three?

Nathaniel sang lustily, *"I always use a seat belt, it keeps me safe and sound. It really is a great belt! It holds me all around!"*

"We're going to Amanda's," she told him.

Nathaniel clapped. He loved Amanda, and her collection of yellow rubber duckies, and especially how Amanda was willing to bob for hours in the shallow end of her pool playing Escape the Sharks.

Lily's cell phone rang.

"It's me, your sister, Rebecca, reminding you before we even start talking not to call me by the nickname I discarded last year, a rule you have not observed even once, and which if you were ever going to give me a gift, it would be to call me Rebecca."

"Give it up, Reb," said Lily, laughing with delight at her sister's voice. "Nobody's ever going to call you Rebecca."

"Please? If I beg and grovel?"

"You've never begged or groveled in your life."

"Today's the day. I'm flying into LaGuardia tonight and I beg you—I'm groveling—can you tell Mom to pick me up at four-thirty? I hate taking the bus."

"You're coming for a visit? How fabulous! I'll come and get you."

"You'd drive into LaGuardia by yourself?" said Reb. "I wouldn't dare."

"Doesn't scare me," said Lily, although it did. It was almost exactly the one-year anniversary of Lily's flight to get Michael. "Mom will be thrilled to see you," she said, trying not to sound reproachful, because after Reb spent Christmas with Freddie, she also spent January break in Texas with Freddie's family. Spring break, Reb went to Florida with friends and, of course, the perfect Freddie. And at the end of Reb's freshman year, just when Mom and Lily were aching to have her around all summer, Reb came home for precisely three days and then caught up with Freddie in Labrador, of all places, where they both had summer jobs.

"Labrador?" Lily had said. "Isn't that awfully far north? Up past Anne of Green Gables?"

"Camping on an ice field," Reb had confirmed. "Are we tough or what?"

Lily was fond of the environment and all that, but she preferred the environment of cities. Freddie and Reb could have the wilderness.

Mom had said sadly, "She likes Freddie's family better."

"She expects them to be different," Lily pointed out. "She didn't expect us to be different."

This was the closest they ever came to discussing that Lily

and Michael had accepted Kells, while Reb had not; that Lily and Michael thought Nathaniel was perfect—which included being perfectly awful—while Reb simply found him awful.

Now her sister said, "Guess why I'm coming home."

"You adore us," said Lily.

"I do. Madly. But why else?"

"You need your laundry done?"

Reb laughed. "I'm coming home to plan my wedding."

O lovely word of white gowns and bright flowers, blaring trumpets and joyful guests. "Reb! I'm so happy for you!" Lily saw a long row of handsome young men in black and white formal garb, their eyes fastened upon the row of beautiful bridesmaids. One of those young men—an intelligent and charming college boy, perhaps with dark hair (Lily warmed to people with dramatic coloring), perhaps a math or engineering major, because Lily had languages and history covered and there was no point in duplicating knowledge—one of those young men would see Lily Victoria Rosetti coming down the aisle, perhaps in rose satin (Reb still liked pink and Lily had begun to accept the pink end of the spectrum), so the flowers would be roses, and shoes—what kind of shoes?—well, anyway, that young man would fall in love with Lily right there in the very same church in which Lily would later marry *him*.

"Will you be my maid of honor?" asked Reb.

"Oh, Reb! Yes!"

✱ ✱ ✱

Mr. Mahanna's boat, the *Saint Anne* (named for Mrs. Mahanna, who told her family loudly and often that she was a saint for putting up with them), had a very powerful engine.

Over the summer, Michael had discovered the joys of fast and loud.

Trey had turned seventeen and lost interest in the expensive power toys he had previously killed Jamie for touching, so Jamie (and therefore Michael) got to use Trey's Jet Skis and ATV. Michael had found that fast and loud could pull you in: you thought no thoughts; you worried no worries. Speed was such an answer.

All summer long, Michael rode his dirtbike over to the Mahannas', where he and Jamie argued fiercely over who got to do what, and because Jamie wanted to be a wrestler when he grew up, this argument was often settled with violence. They took corners too fast and fell off things and got gravel stuck in their torn kneecaps. Jamie loved a good wound and was always hoping for streams of blood.

Michael and Jamie had classmates whose parents never even let them be alone in a toy store, never mind on bikes five miles from home. They had acquaintances whose only excitement in life was on a video screen and knew one boy who had never done a single thing outdoors: never fallen or tripped or bled; never even got dirty.

Mr. Mahanna let Michael drive the boat first while Jamie yelled that it wasn't fair, which it wasn't, and when Jamie finally got a turn, Michael sat with Trey. "Your new fourth-grade teacher?" Trey yelled over the engine. "I had the same teacher when I was in fourth! I loved fourth grade!"

Michael was always astonished when people claimed to love school. Michael's crowd—not Jamie, of course; the Mahannas were perfect—were always getting tutored or remediated. They had to be "brought up to speed" or given some "one-on-one." You never loved that kind of school. You showed up and eventually it ended.

Jamie wanted to motor up to Plum Island, where scientists studied infectious animal diseases. Jamie had heard that if you landed on the island, they had to shoot you because you were now a carrier of death. Jamie wanted to penetrate the island's defenses or at least find out whether the scientists shot blanks or real bullets.

"You guys are lucky enough you've got a Teacher Work Day, whatever that is," said Mr. Mahanna. "Even luckier that I can take the day off. And now you also want the joys of being shot at? Forget it."

Trey opened a bag of Cheez Doodles for himself and tossed Michael the Fluff and peanut butter sandwich Mrs. Mahanna had made just for him.

My own father doesn't know I love Fluff, thought Michael. Doesn't know I'm pretty much okay in fourth. That I read almost at grade level. That I can drive a boat.

Michael had largely unmemorized the two and a half weeks spent with his father. But now and then a piece of the visit would spew forth, getting him in the eyes like chlorinated water from a pool. He remembered the testing at that new school where Dad had put him. How scornfully the principal had considered Michael's scores. "Your son needs a special class," he had said, and Dad had shot a look of shame and anger at the son who was stupid.

Michael was as smart as anybody else. But he could not scrape knowledge up off the page the way all the girls and most of the boys could. It just lay there, stuck in little black shapes on white paper, and he couldn't get hold of it.

Michael held the uneaten Fluff sandwich and stared out to sea.

Then he unmemorized his father. It was too bad school didn't require unlearning. He was a whiz.

* * *

Lily opened the high, difficult latch of the gate that protected Amanda's swimming pool from marauding toddlers. Amanda lay flat on her chaise, her bare back facing the sun, her eyes closed.

What a contrast their lives were. Amanda's so slow and leisurely; Lily's so frantic and full. What if Amanda continued to be comfortable in the sun, doing nothing much, while Lily joined the footrace that was city life? What if their friendship dwindled away, like Lily's friendship with her very own sister—and only one of them noticed?

"Hi, Amanda!" shrieked Nathaniel, attacking.

Amanda rolled over and swept him up, hugging and kissing. "Hello, most perfect short person in the universe."

"Can I put the rubber duckies in the water?"

"You can. They're in their net bag. See it hanging over there?"

Nathaniel hurried to the fence where the rubber duckies hung. The hook was too high for him. It never occurred to him to ask for help. He dragged over a chair to stand on.

"Great news," said Lily, rubbing sunscreen into a forgotten spot on Amanda's back. "Reb is coming home tonight to plan her wedding to Freddie!"

As always, Amanda reacted perfectly. "Do I get to go to the bridal showers and the parties? I want to be part of all the shopping. When is the wedding? Next June?"

"Who knows? Who cares? I'm just glad they're not eloping. It would be just like Reb to hop in a canoe and meet a justice of the peace at some bend in the river."

"Remember the first time we saw a photograph of Freddie," said Amanda, "and I wanted to steal him? The guy is movie-star quality. What did Reb ever do to deserve him?"

Lily didn't care whether anybody deserved anything. Love was beautiful, Reb was beautiful, the wedding would be beautiful.

"Doesn't Freddie have a brother?" asked Amanda. "I'm sure I remember an e-mail from Reb discussing the brother of Freddie. He'll be best man, and I totally bet it turns out he's *really* the best man—for you."

They giggled. "I cannot marry Freddie's brother. I refuse to be Mrs. Crumb."

"His last name is *Crumb*?"

"Yup. Reb's kids will be the little Crumbs."

"A good case for keeping your own name," agreed Amanda. "Why don't you leave Nathaniel with me for dinner as well? It might be easier than hauling him to the airport and dealing with him when you're trying to have a reunion with Reb."

Lily shook her head. "He sees so little of Reb and Reb so little of him. And he's perfect these days, so I'll bring him."

Amanda raised her eyebrows.

"Well, perfect with lapses," Lily admitted.

"Hourly lapses," Amanda pointed out.

Nathaniel had gotten the bag down. Amanda strapped a swim vest around his waist and over his shoulders and lifted him in her arms. She walked out on the diving board over the deep end and bounced hard. On the second bounce, they cannonballed.

Nathaniel came up sputtering and shouting, "Again! Again!"

He had already forgotten Lily, who slipped out the gate and headed for work. She knew perfectly well that it was a bad plan to take Nathaniel to the airport. He'd be so exhausted by an afternoon playing hard with Amanda that he'd have tantrums.

But a person in charge of somebody else had to be brave,

and that person was braver with somebody holding her hand, and a person going to the airport for the first time in almost fifty-two weeks—that person might need a hand to hold.

"Doctors Bence, Alzina and Gladwin," said Lily over and over. It was extra busy since kids didn't have school, so emergencies and problems had been wedged in left and right. Lily normally worked only three to five-thirty. Today she was working ten to four, and the place was insane.

"Don't worry about missing Kelsey's appointment, Mrs. Smith," she would say. "Schedules are so busy these days." Although everybody's day was busy and *they* got here, so what was Kelsey's mother's problem? Then she would yell across the room. "Conor, brushing your teeth for six seconds doesn't count. It has to be the full two minutes.

"No, Conor. You won't die of toothpaste poisoning if you keep the toothpaste in your mouth the full two minutes."

And then, because it was Conor, who reminded her of Michael once and Nathaniel now, she'd yell, "Fine! Drop dead! But you'll never get your braces checked and you'll never be able to leave the office and they'll lock up and you'll be rotting on the floor in here while other people are enjoying their Thursday off from school!"

When Lily got back to Amanda's, Nathaniel was sound asleep on an air mattress in the shade. Amanda was standing against the pool enclosure, backlit by the sun. Shimmering light framed her fair hair. She wore a long silky robe and gleamed like some ancient seer or oracle. And then, almost regally, almost ceremonially, Amanda took Lily's hand.

How strange it felt: escorted to a seat by the cool hand of her friend.

Amanda arranged herself on the seat across from Lily. She was clearly also arranging her thoughts. "Lily," she said carefully. "You'll be your sister's maid of honor. I've been thinking all day what that means. I want to withdraw our prayer."

There was only one prayer to which Lily had eagerly cried *Amen.*

No matter how many times you said or sang *Amen,* the word never felt English. It came from Latin, which took it from Greek, which took it from Hebrew. It meant "truly" or, in the King James Version, "verily." A word for when you agreed. But the Lord evidently hadn't agreed, because denrose was still alive and kicking. (Actually, Lily had no first-hand knowledge of this, but his address still occupied its place in Reb's e-mail list. Surely if Reb had gone to denrose's funeral, she would have mentioned it.)

I bet we're dead for denrose, thought Lily. I bet at parties when other people refer to their children, he says, "I never had kids myself."

Amanda looked away from Lily and stared up into the sky, first from one angle, then from another, frowning slightly.

"Looking for God?" said Lily.

"I'd love a glimpse," agreed Amanda. "God!" she yelled in her demanding way. "I'm sorry!" she shouted at Him. She flopped back down on her chaise while Lily continued to study the sky for results.

"Toss me the sunscreen," said Amanda.

Lily handed it over.

"Because the thing is," said Amanda, "your father will be at Reb's wedding."

chapter 11

That man—whose name Lily wouldn't even say out loud—at the wedding? *That man* walking Reb down the aisle—as if he deserved the title "father"?

It was unthinkable that he would saunter back into their lives, walk his elder daughter down the aisle, shake hands with every guest as if he were an actual father. He would upstage Kells, because anybody could, and here it was Kells who had been the good guy. Michael would be forced to stand next to denrose.

So many parents got surprised by their own children: by their size or the lack of it; by their brains or the lack of them; by their hobbies and interests and passions or the lack of them. Parents who thought sports were stupid had children who were athletic stars. Parents who despised technology had children who solved the school's computer problems in third grade. Parents who listened only to hard rock had children who practiced Mozart.

But only Dad, surprised by Michael, threw his child away.

When Dad looked in a mirror, he must see that handsome tanned man, blue eyes like a husky dog, the half smile that captivated strangers, those trendy clothes and fine wristwatch. But he would never see what Michael had seen: his back.

Lily had never been able to imagine the actual thinking of the actual parent as he actually drove to an airport, actually opened his own car door, actually left his eight-year-old on the sidewalk and actually departed.

She had not been to LaGuardia since that day. How amazing that only Lily (possibly Michael, but eight-year-olds had little grasp of the calendar) knew that the anniversary was at hand. Early September had two anniversaries for the rest of America: Labor Day and September 11. Only Lily had her very own date burned inside her. She believed she had become stronger and deeper from that terrible event, but not strong and deep enough for this.

I'm not praying to you, she informed God. You never come through. I'm working this out for myself. So there! (As if God would be threatened by the loss of Lily's prayers.) And then, because there was nowhere else to turn, she said anyway, *God. Don't let me be this angry. It's my sister. Let me love Reb the way I love Nathaniel. The way families are supposed to love. Let me not go crazy with rage at Reb just because she wants her father in her wedding. But don't let him come. Don't you let my father hurt Michael again!*

"Sunscreen?" asked Amanda.

"No, thanks," said Lily, "I'd better wake Nathaniel up and head for LaGuardia." She was nervous.

It was one thing to be a new driver locally, on plain old roads and intersections she'd known all her life as a passenger. It was quite another to conquer the complex circles and merges, short-term and long-term parking entrances and exits, departure lanes and security blockades of LaGuardia Airport.

Carefully Amanda lifted the little hot body under his towel-blanket and kissed Nathaniel's sweaty little forehead. Together the girls tilted him into his car seat without waking him. "Thanks," said Lily.

"My pleasure," said Amanda, and Lily thought: It really is her pleasure. *Why, why, wasn't Michael a pleasure to Dad?*

But surely this was the question Michael had asked himself a thousand times.

Rage swelled in Lily again, making her fingers so stiff she could hardly close them around the steering wheel. When she made a right turn, her arms were unyielding, as if she were holding off an attack. I'm having an anger seizure, she thought. I should stop driving.

Naturally she accelerated instead.

Speed was a wonderful thing. Going straight through the red light would be so satisfying. Lily shoved her foot to the floor. She didn't care what happened. It would serve everybody right if—

"Wiwwy," called Nathaniel from the backseat, "I see Dunkin' Donuts! Can I have a jewwy doughnut?"

She had forgotten Nathaniel. The thing she most held against her father—forgetting his children—and she herself had done it. Lily braked mentally and physically and turned into Dunkin' Donuts.

"Not the drive-in," pleaded Nathaniel, who always wanted to go indoors and be part of the action. So they got out of the car and at the counter she lifted him up so he could take in all the exciting doughnut sights. "Two doughnuts?" begged

Nathaniel, his brown eyes wide with anxiety. It was a lot to ask.

She nodded and gave him the money to pay. Nathaniel loved to pay. "Two jewwy doughnuts, pwease," he said proudly. "Are we weaving a tip, Wiwwy?" he whispered. Nathaniel loved tipping. She handed him a quarter, but Nathaniel was a big tipper. He wanted to leave two quarters. "Can I have coffee, Wiwwy?"

"You're too little."

"Sometimes," said the counter girl, "we give kids a half inch of coffee and fill the cup up with milk."

Lily relented. Nathaniel held his coffee like treasure, proud to sip from the hole in the lid like a grown-up. In the car, he protected his doughnuts and coffee from seat belt damage and they headed to LaGuardia.

Lily concentrated on every difficult turn and confusing road arrangement, reading the signs that came and went so quickly, grateful that Nathaniel was preoccupied balancing his coffee. He seemed not to notice the planes landing and taking off until they were right inside the airport complex, jammed between a construction site and a parking garage. A plane skimmed over their heads and Nathaniel shouted, "Wiwwy! *We* went onna pane that time!"

That Nathaniel should remember an event that took place one-third of his life ago! She saw him again, little legs churning, as he rushed to his big brother and proved to Michael that love still lived. He had saved Michael from two things: hopelessness and a shoplifting charge.

"We went onna pane," said Nathaniel to himself, because Michael and Lily had never backed him up and his daddy and mommy had never listened.

Through her tears Lily saw Reb on the sidewalk, tall and slim and beautiful and soon to be a bride! When Lily pulled up next to the curb, Reb said, "Lily, I didn't know you missed me enough to cry! I should have come home more."

Yes, thought Lily, you should.

She vaulted out of the car, ran around and hugged Reb hard, convinced that everything would be all right. "Pop the trunk," ordered Reb, lifting her suitcases.

It didn't take much to jumpstart the old nightmare. The moment her fingertips encountered the handle of a suitcase, Lily knew she was doomed to dream it again tonight.

It was absurd, since she and Michael and Nathaniel had not had a piece of luggage among them. But in the dream, security guards and police and flight attendants and passing strangers screamed, *"Where's your luggage? Where's Michael?"* and Lily had no answer, because she never found Michael. She would look for Nathaniel and see that he was gone too; she held only an arm.

Reb slid into the passenger seat and leaned between the front seats to kiss Nathaniel. "Aaaaaaaah! I forgot little boys are sticky and disgusting!"

"Jewwy doughnut, Reb," said Nathaniel, beaming. Generously, he held out a mangled well-licked handful.

Reb looked at Lily. "He hasn't changed."

"No," agreed Lily. "He's still perfect." She and Reb would stay up all night talking weddings and Lily would avoid having the nightmare by never going to sleep to start with.

When Mom had admired every single thing about Reb and finished singing for joy at this unexpected visit, she went into a flurry of self-improvement, madly picking up mail-order catalogs that had slid to the floor and sticking sweaters on hangers and rushing into the kitchen for a cooking spree. While she waltzed around measuring and dicing and stirring and beaming at Reb, Lily set the table. "What can I do?" asked Reb.

"You just sit there and be home," said Mom, dancing. "I am so so so so happy to see you, darling!"

"I fix supper too, Reb," Nathaniel told her. "I do water!" He never tired of pushing a glass against the automatic ice crusher in the refrigerator door, but as usual he got excited and pushed too long. Ice shot everywhere. Reb mopped up the floor with paper towels and said, "Nathaniel? Want to be a ring bearer?"

Nathaniel was the only kid in history who never went through a "No!" stage. "Yes!" he shouted, because Nathaniel agreed to anything anytime suggested by anybody. Lily figured he was a good candidate for kidnapping because he'd be so eager for the excursion.

Mom paused mid–tomato slice. Ring bearer was a position that didn't come up often. "Does Nathaniel want *what*?"

"Ring bearer. Freddie and I are getting married. I'm home to plan our wedding."

Joy drained out of Mom's face. Shock took over. "*What?* You're nineteen! You're far too young."

"Mom, be grateful there's going to be a marriage at all. Freddie and I could just live together. That's what everybody else does."

Mom was frantic. She dropped the knife and the tomato and held her hands out, making a stop sign. "I don't want you getting married young! I want you to live in exciting cities and stake out a great career and establish yourself! I want you to create a space on earth that's yours and yours alone."

Reb shook her head. "I don't want a space for me, Mom.

I want a space for *us*. You know that Freddie is three years older than I am. You know he graduated last June. Well, the company we worked for in Labrador gave him a permanent job. Petroleum engineers go everywhere, Mom. I'll see the world following Freddie."

"Following!" Mom approved of band members following a conductor, but she did not approve of women following their men. "You're a language major, Rebbie. I want you to get a graduate degree or go into diplomacy, or—or—or at least import Italian shoes."

Lily giggled.

"Shoes are good," agreed Reb. "Let's talk about shoes. And wedding gowns. We can look for wedding gowns Friday. Tomorrow, Saturday, is my appointment with Dr. Bordon. I'm there to firm up the date for the church—October twenty-fourth—and he wants to talk about Christian commitment or something. Then you and I find a place for the reception, call the florist and it's a wrap." Reb beamed.

Mom seemed unable to balance. She braced herself against the butcher block.

Cautiously, Lily said, "You don't mean *this* October twenty-fourth, do you, Reb?" Lily had read her share of brides' magazines. It took two years to pull off a wedding.

Reb tap-danced around the kitchen table. Lily had forgotten that Reb had studied tap all through middle school and had only given it up when she got into swimming and water polo. How easy to forget things, even about somebody you loved.

"Freddie's getting specialized training at the New York office," explained Reb, "which ends October twenty-first, and then it's back to Labrador, so October twenty-fourth is the only reasonable Saturday."

"But Reb," Mom protested, "you'd have to rush down

here from college, rush through a wedding, and rush back to class. You mustn't get married now, Reb, but when you do, don't shove your wedding into a corner. June after your college graduation—three years from now—is the earliest you could possibly have this wedding."

"Oh," said Reb casually. She took a position on the safe side of the kitchen table. She tilted her body like a model in a magazine displaying casual wear. "Well. Actually, Mom. I quit college."

In Lily's family, this was a sin right up there with ungodliness. You went to college, you excelled, you graduated. Mom herself had a bachelor's degree. She had raised her children to believe that a master's was the very least they should settle for, and a doctorate, or being a doctor, was better. "No," said Mom flatly. "You have to finish your degree, Rebecca."

Reb shook her head, sweeping her long hair back and forth like a ten-year-old saying *Nuh-uh*. "Freddie and I were so close this summer, Mother. Up in Labrador, camping under the stars! When I got back to school two weeks ago, I was miserable, and so was he. If we don't get married, we won't see each other for months. You can see that's impossible."

Mom was screaming now. "You cannot drop out of college!"

Nathaniel's chin quivered. He didn't often hear raised voices, and they upset him. He wasn't afraid of swimming pools or planes, but he was afraid of anger.

Me too, thought Lily. And I have more of it than anybody. She picked him up and he buried his face in her shoulder.

"I can quit, Mom," said Reb. "And I have. They've offered me a job at the base camp too. They need somebody for computer entries."

"You're going to be a *clerk*? Doing data entry for a bunch of engineers?" shrieked Mom, and of course this was one of the problems with Freddie—he wasn't mapping where pods of sweet old whales swam; he was mapping where oil rigs could be established. Politically correct environmentalists they weren't.

Reb assumed a bright cheerful expression. "Let's talk about *your* dress, Mom! What a beautiful mother of the bride you'll be."

In her dangerous voice, the one that meant she would just as soon iron Reb's skin as her shirt, Mom said, "Finish your degree, Rebecca. *Then* have the wedding."

But Reb had inherited that very voice. "I'd like to live here until the wedding, Mother, but I could just as easily live with Freddie's family and have the wedding in Texas."

Whoa, thought Lily. Serious blackmail. Lily stepped in to give Mom time to chill. "No honeymoon, Reb? That schedule sounds pretty tight."

"My entire life will be a honeymoon."

"There's no such thing," snapped Mom. "Nineteen is not old enough to know your mind, Reb. It's too easy to make a mistake."

"Do not bring your failed marriage into this, Mother. I do not plan to ruin my marriage the way you ruined yours."

* * *

When dinner was in the oven, and Lily had fixed iced tea and Reb and Mom were stirring their tea and pretending they still liked each other, Reb produced a bride's magazine. "Look!" she said to Nathaniel. "This is what you'll wear at my wedding."

In an all-white shot—white carpet, walls and flowers—

a tiny blond boy in short white pants, white bowtie and white dinner jacket simpered over a white velvet pillow.

"Aaaaaaaagh!" screamed Nathaniel, quite reasonably, Lily thought. "No!" he said, a rare word for him.

"Nathaniel, you'll be adorable," Reb protested.

"I wouldn't wear that on Hawwoween," Nathaniel told her.

"How old is this kid?" demanded Reb. "There's something wrong with the water in this house. Michael acts thirty-five, and now Nathaniel thinks he's in seventh grade. It wouldn't be the end of the world to dress like that," she told Nathaniel.

"*You* do it, then," he said.

Reb looked at her family as if they were roadkill. In Freddie's family, people would be enthusiastic and three-year-olds would know their place. "On Saturday," she said, and kindly enlarged on this for any unintelligent people in the room, "which is tomorrow, Freddie is coming out by train. He will meet me at the church. I'll bring him back here for lunch, Mother. Please make an effort to be nice."

"I'm always nice," said their mother, not nicely.

Lily giggled. "We'll be nice, Reb. What do you want to eat? Is Freddie something annoying, like a fruititarian, or can we get pepperoni sausage pizza?"

"We are not ordering pizza for the very first time Freddie meets you! I want you to make a good impression."

Mom looked like a bull in Spain. A stabbed bull. Because Reb didn't care what Mom thought about Freddie; she cared what Freddie thought about Mom. Mom was on trial.

I can't let them say anything more, thought Lily. Especially when the real fight is yet to come.

The sound of the front door opening interrupted everything.

"Daddy's here!" shrieked Nathaniel happily, racing out of the kitchen. "Daddy, guess what?"

Lily hoped Reb would be nice to Kells. Reb always seemed faintly surprised he existed. But for once, Reb looked cheerful, perhaps knowing that Nathaniel would spill everything—his big sister was here! getting married! having a wedding! needing a ring bearer!

"Daddy," said Nathaniel breathlessly, "we went where we went in the pane that time."

"You never went in a plane," said his father, laughing.

Kells came into the kitchen with Nathaniel riding on his shoulders, Nathaniel's favorite place in the whole world, saw Reb and grinned. "What a great surprise! Rebecca, what brings you home? I'm so happy to see you!"

"She *thinks* she's getting *married* in six weeks," began Mom, "but—"

Kells crossed the room and bent over Reb to kiss her while Nathaniel screamed in delight at the risk of falling off. "Congratulations," said Kells. "You'll be a beautiful bride."

It didn't please Reb that her stepfather was the one who said the right thing.

He's always been the one who says the right thing, thought Lily.

When Dad had left, several years ago, largely from boredom at having to be so suburban and maintain a family and a mortgage, Mom had been devastated. She pleaded with Dennis to come back, promising any concession. But Dad was in love with the word "divorce" the way Reb was now in love with the word "wedding." Dad laughed out loud at the idea that he would return to anything as confining as a family when he could live alone and make no compromises or effort.

When it was Mom who fell in love, six months later, the entire family was astonished and offended, but the most astonished and the most offended was the one who had left: Dad. When he couldn't change things by throwing insults ("You *like* that stupid fat bore?"), Dennis Rosetti moved out of state.

All three of Dennis Rosetti's children held the stupid fat bore responsible. Lily and Michael had gotten over it. Reb had not.

So Reb smiled tightly at Kells and said nothing to him. "Help me unpack, Lily?"

Lily carried the heaviest suitcase and felt the dream drawing itself up, like enemy troops. The front hall, stairs and upstairs hall were filled with stuff: Christmas decorations that had never gotten boxed; winter clothes that had never reached the dry cleaner's; paperbacks waiting to be exchanged at the used-book store; little shirts Nathaniel had outgrown over the summer, or even last spring.

They went into Reb's old bedroom. Mom had started using it for overflow. Piles of litter oozed toward Reb's old bed.

"I didn't miss this chaos," said Reb. "My dorm room is so neat, people at school call me the Cleaning Woman."

"How did your roommate handle that?"

"I explained to her the first day what the rules were."

"Sort of like God," said Lily.

Reb giggled and flung her arms around Lily, and they tap-danced together.

"Oh, Reb," whispered Lily. "I'm so happy for you. I'm so glad you love Freddie so much and that he loves you."

"His family is perfect," said Reb. "If only we had a family like that."

Lily stiffened. "We do."

Reb stepped away. She threw a suitcase on the bed and unzipped it vigorously. She had even packed neatly, every sock rolled up with its partner. But she didn't touch the contents. She folded her arms and spoke. "Now that we're alone, we need to have a crucial conversation, Lily. You have issues with Dad, which I don't pretend to understand. It's time to get over it. You have to grow up. Dad and I are very close. We talk on the phone all the time. He's thrilled with my decision to marry Freddie next month, and after going camping with us twice this summer, Dad loves Freddie as much as I do."

What? thought Lily. He *what*? Michael gets nothing, while some boyfriend of Reb's is Dad's new best friend?

"You have tried to destroy our family, Lily. I haven't pressed you about your motives. I do not think there's any point discussing what's already happened. But from now on, you have to behave."

I have to behave? How dare—

"Lily," said Reb, "Dad will be giving me away. I can't put my real family back together and there's nothing I can do about Kells, but I can do something about the people who matter. I need you to telephone Dad tonight and apologize for cutting him out of your life. Right now, this evening over dinner, you stop poisoning Michael against him. Admit your role in this, Lily, and help Michael be friends with Dad again too."

Lily could not breathe.

"My wedding is going to be perfect," said Reb.

"Rebecca," said Lily, and she knew she would never use her sister's nickname again because a nickname was affectionate, "you invite that snake and I won't be at that wedding."

They stared at each other across a pink bedspread and a littered carpet.

"You ruin my wedding day and I will never forgive you," said her sister. Rebecca walked out of the room and down the stairs.

Lily was acquainted with never forgiving.

It lasted a long time.

chapter

12

In spite of a wonderful day out on the water, Michael was filled with dread. He should never have let himself remember. It would just lead to another Dad sighting. He would see Dad coming out of a store or climbing into a car. It would be all he could do not to race after the guy. He would imagine himself leaping whole flights of stairs, jumping from high windows—anything to catch up.

Every time it happened, it was real, even when it wasn't. Who would have thought a Fluff sandwich could do this to him? Michael schooled himself to the sober courtesy that helped him stay emotionless. "Thank you for a wonderful day, Mr. Mahanna. See you, Jamie. Bye, Trey." Michael got into the car with his stepfather and decided not to look out the window during the drive home. He examined his knees.

"Got a surprise at home, Michael," said Kells, driving in his leisurely way, two fingertips on the wheel. "A very unexpected visitor."

All thought and breath left Michael. *Dad! Dad's here.* Kells didn't joke or tease, so this was a fact. Dad was here.

To think Michael had wasted time with Jamie! How long would Dad stay? How much of the visit had Michael missed? This time Michael would get it right. This time—

"Rebecca's home from college," said Kells.

Michael willed himself not to cry, but soaked up his own tears like a paper towel.

Kells turned into their street. Rebecca was out in the yard waiting for them. She was tall and thin, waving both arms high in the air, but her feet were motionless. Rebecca could always stand as if she went right down into the ground like a fence post. As if nothing could move her.

He thought of his father all the time, but rarely of his older sister. Yet she was the reason for it all. It was not until she was leaving for college that Michael had understood that a person could live somewhere else. He had the blinding, brilliant knowledge that he too could go away—but not to college—*he* could live with *Dad.* He had phoned Dad, listing all the advantages and the things they would do together. It took several calls to convince Dad. Michael had promised not to be any trouble.

He had broken the promise.

As soon as Michael was out of the car, Rebecca kissed him hard and then shoved him away to look him up and down and yanked him back for hugs and then did it again. It was like a whipsaw ride at the county fair. "You're so tall!" she cried. "I'm so glad to see you! You're hardly even a little boy anymore. You're practically a teenager!"

He nodded.

"It's a good thing you never took over my bedroom, Michael, because I'm home for a while. Guess why I'm home."

"You live here," he said. He had almost forgotten what she looked like. She looked perfect.

"Freddie and I are getting married," his sister said, and she smiled the widest, happiest smile in the world, and he was helpless; he smiled back. "I'm home to plan the wedding."

Weddings were what grown-ups did.

My sister is a grown-up, thought Michael.

"You'll be in a tuxedo," said Reb, "the one who ushers Mom to her seat, and when I marry Freddie, you'll be right there, smiling at me."

He had been at a wedding once. When Mom married Kells. It hadn't been the kind with a church aisle and a long white dress. It was just family and friends in the backyard with the minister. Michael remembered the barbecue better than the wedding.

Nathaniel barreled out of the house and squeezed between Michael and Rebecca. He couldn't stand it when Michael paid attention to anybody else. He had a magazine picture to show Michael and Michael tried to avoid this, but Rebecca wanted him to look too, so he stared down at the photograph of a too-pretty little boy in white.

"Nathaniel will be the ring bearer," said Rebecca. "Dressed just like that."

Michael laughed. "Forget it," he advised his little brother.

★ ★ ★

Since the second week in September was just right for eating outside, Kells lit the candles that were supposed to keep away the mosquitoes and Mom rallied and even located some dusty crystal bowls and filled them with water and floated flowers in them.

Over dinner, Rebecca told them about Freddie and Labrador and Texas while Nathaniel shouted to be heard and Kells asked all the right questions. Mom said safe things like did anybody want more ketchup. What power people had over each other. Lily could still remember her father's threats—"I'm going to leave this family!" he'd shout. And then he did. People usually did what they said, in Lily's experience. So Rebecca might well leave too. Whatever Rebecca dished out, Mom would have to take with a smile, or lose her.

"Lily, dear," said Mom, who never called her Lily, dear, "will you get the ice cream?"

Lily went back into the kitchen. She decided on the bright red dessert bowls because Mom loved them. She put on a large tray all four kinds of ice cream she found in the freezer, the bowls, spoons, the ice cream scoop, extra napkins and a bag of cookies. Carefully she maneuvered toward the table.

"Guess what, Michael," said Rebecca.

Don't do this to us, Rebecca, thought Lily. Michael cannot handle it. It will smack him in the forehead like a baseball. Pieces of nightmare split and multiplied in Lily's head like viruses.

"Michael," said Rebecca. "Dad's coming for the wedding."

A smile Lily had not seen in months spread across Michael's face. He began laughing in an extraordinary bursting sort of way, as if joy were coming out of his pores.

"Dad?" he repeated. "Dad's coming?" Jumping to his feet, throwing his arms around Reb, he cried, *"Dad's coming?"*

Reb was beaming and laughing and they hugged each other and rocked back and forth and said over and over, "Yes! Dad's coming!"

Twelve months of not hearing Dad's voice on the phone.

One full year without so much as a card for his birthday.

A year without Christmas.

A year in which his father never asked to see a report card or to have a photograph of his only son.

And Michael didn't care.

Dad was coming.

Michael still thinks his father is perfect, thought Lily. He still wants to please Dad. It's like wanting to please God. You're never going to hear from Him, so why bother? Yet if you believe, you're always bothering.

Rebecca and Lily did not talk through the night. They did not talk at all. By choice, Lily did not pray. She knew how terrible her prayer would be—for violence against Dennis. Meanwhile, Michael would pray for love and the opposing prayers might slam into each other and get tangled and make it all worse.

Friday morning, school felt thin and pointless, sandwiched between that Teacher Work Day and a weekend Lily now dreaded. At lunch she shrugged about the class schedule she was supposed to follow, found Amanda and told her everything.

In her heart, Lily knew Amanda was a lonely person. Her

life only looked perfect. Her brilliant, wonderful parents worked twelve hours a day, including commutes, and Amanda had essentially brought herself up. She was fine with it, but what she wanted for herself was a house like Lily's: busy, noisy and chaotic, with little boys to hug and read aloud to.

Amanda, like Rebecca, just wanted to get married. She wanted the husband and the home and children they would have together, and all the demands and the privileges these meant. Amanda didn't care about a career. Lily felt the reverse. She'd already been the parent, both to Michael and to Nathaniel. Lily craved the demands and privileges of life on her own.

Amanda said, "Did you keep the bill for the airline tickets?"

After the credit card bill arrived, Lily had gone to the bank and emptied her savings account and the bank had written its own check to the credit card company. Since she'd gone to a branch Mom and Kells didn't use, Lily was unknown to the bank, and all it was, was a transaction. The teller hardly noticed it going by. Then Lily canceled the credit card. "I kept the bill," Lily told Amanda.

"So show it to them. That backs up your story."

Lily's lunch tray was old. The plastic sides had gotten frizzled in the dishwashers and the edges rubbed against her palms like sandpaper. She didn't take any food off the tray. Hunger seemed distant and unknown. "It's Michael's story to tell if he wants to. And he doesn't want to."

"So what?" said Amanda. "If Rebecca wants her father at her wedding, that's her privilege. But nobody should be confused about the kind of guy Dennis is. No matter what Michael thinks, you need to tell, because Michael can't go off with this guy again. And that could possibly happen."

Trey Mahanna slid into the chair next to Amanda, facing

Lily. "Hi," he said, interested, because he knew perfectly well this was not in fact her lunch period.

Lily mustered a fake smile. "Hi."

"So he's coming to the wedding," said Trey.

The girls gaped at him.

"Michael called Jamie right away," Trey explained. "Michael's thrilled."

Lily hated it that all these perfect people—Trey's family, Freddie's family, Amanda's family—knew the flaws in Lily's; they were following her story like a soap opera. They had their favorite characters; they knew what episode they wanted next.

"Lily," said Trey, looking awkward and nervous, "was the thing that your father did to Michael—was it like—well—sexual? Because my father says that—"

"No!" whispered Lily. "It was not! Don't you dare repeat or think or say such a thing. Don't you dare make things worse, Trey Mahanna. You and your father stay out of this!" It took such effort to keep her voice down. She was sorry she hadn't crushed Trey with a chair last year in Anger Management. Maybe right now she'd flip the table on him and smash his questioning jaw. "Stop speculating," she hissed at him. "Stop trying to be helpful. *Just stop.*"

* * *

Lily worked at the orthodontists' that afternoon, her usual hours, three to five-thirty. Her job was to carry out cheerful little chores in a cheerful little way and she pulled it off until four-fifteen, when she looked up to see Trey.

"I have an appointment," he mumbled, not meeting her eyes.

"We're running a few minutes late," she said stiffly. "Please have a seat."

He chose an alcove where they wouldn't have to look at each other.

Lily never entered the treatment room when Trey was the patient. It was okay for some eleven-year-old to be all splayed out, mouth propped open, chairside assistant sucking up saliva. It was not okay for some seventeen-year-old, especially not a boy you knew. Middle school kids liked being part of the orthodonture crowd; it was like some subdued anxious club. High school students loathed it. She glanced at Trey's record. It was a long appointment. Trey was getting his braces off.

At five-fifteen, Dr. Alzina requested that Lily take Trey's After photos. There were always two: one to staple to the record and another to staple to the bulletin board where little signs proclaimed YAY! CONGRATS! YOU LOOK AWESOME!

Trey was waiting in the little blue hall with the bright lights where Lily would snap his picture. He didn't look at her. She lifted the Polaroid camera. "Your teeth have to be in the photograph, Trey."

"Huh?"

"You have to smile. That's the point of all this suffering. Smiling."

"What do I get in return?"

"I tell you how handsome you are."

He grinned and she quickly took his picture. Slowly the photograph slid out, firmed up and got clear. "Trey, you are a total doll. Look at those teeth. You are so handsome."

"You get paid to say that."

"True," said Lily. Really true in your case, she thought. "All Afters look great, though," she told him. "I love how every Before really and truly does become an After."

Dr. Alzina had rooted around in Trey's records to get the photo from before he got braces. Trey looked awful. Receding chin, overlapping teeth, sticking-out teeth, one extra deformed tooth and a look of terror. The whole staff crowded around, as was the custom to celebrate Afters. "Trey, you're such a hunk!" cried the receptionist.

"I'm in love with you," said the insurance clerk.

Dr. Alzina photographed Lily smiling at Trey's Before and After.

"Can I keep that one?" asked Trey.

"Sure," said Dr. Alzina. Then he got interested. "You two an item? Orthodonture romance. It's the best." He focused the camera on both of them. "Give us a kiss."

"We haven't had our first kiss yet," said Trey.

"What's the matter with you?" said Dr. Alzina. "Pick up the pace."

* * *

When the last patient was gone, Lily still had to clean up. It was her turn to do the patients' bathroom. She slid on disposable gloves, swabbed sink and toilet and found her poise going straight down the toilet with the cleanser. She could be the dutiful employee here, all cheerful and smooth, but once she got home, she'd be the middle child who was nothing but a threat to her brother and sister.

When she finally got to her car, there in her front passenger seat sat Trey Mahanna. Lily got in the driver's side, slid behind the wheel and put the key in the ignition. "Yes?" she said.

"I'm not an ordinary After," said Trey.

He spoke the truth. He was an extraordinary After. Not

only was he good-looking, but like his father, he was nice all the way through. All the way down. All through the years. But Lily did not want to be nice. She hated being nice. How come it wasn't other people's turn to be nice to her?

Jesus, Jesus, she said to Him. When I'm paid I can be nice. But I can't be nice to family. I can't be nice to Trey. And I sure can't be nice to Dennis Rosetti. Oh, Jesus, I feel as if I'm running to a place where I never want to arrive. The place where I'll hate my sister. Jesus, don't let it happen.

"Want to go to a movie tonight?" asked Trey.

"I'm busy."

He sat very still.

Jesus, Lily continued, I want to love people. But they have to make it easier. People are so annoying and they never go away when they should.

Jesus was definitely amused. Lily could tell.

"What's funny?" said Trey.

"God."

"Are you swearing at me or answering?"

"Answering. God is funny. The way He does or does not show up." She was going to sob now. She was not going to do this in front of Trey Mahanna. "Does Jesus ever actually help you?" she asked him. "Are you ever actually nicer to people because of Jesus?"

Trey got out of her car. He shut the door. He leaned back in the window. "I'm nice to you, aren't I? If that doesn't take the help of God, I don't know what does."

chapter
13

When Lily finally got home from the orthodontists', the house was completely quiet.

She peeked in the family room. Kells was asleep in his recliner in front of a silent television, Nathaniel snoozing in his arms.

She tiptoed into the kitchen and saw a note taped to the refrigerator, because everyone in the family opened the refrigerator door upon returning from anything. Lily hardly ever snacked, but she always liked to assess what was available.

Mom and I are at the bridal mall, said the note. *Home for dinner. A million things to tell everybody. Rebecca.*

Lily wrenched the note off the door, screwed it up in her

hand and flung it at the trash can. They had gone wedding gown shopping without her? It was her own fault. How could they take her to the bridal mall when she had refused to be in the wedding?

"Hi," said Michael.

She would never get used to how silent he was. It was like living with a cat. Every now and then you heard the slightest patter of feet or a purr. Otherwise, his presence was unknown to you.

"They went wedding gown shopping without me," blurted Lily, when she would have liked to shout, *How can you possibly be glad you'll see that snake again?* but Michael, being a boy, didn't understand the meaning of this and just opened the refrigerator door, no doubt grateful *he* hadn't been taken shopping. "There's chocolate pudding," he suggested.

"It isn't real," said Lily. "It's in those little plastic cups." Lily liked cooked pudding with the skin on the top.

"I'll make real pudding," Michael offered.

"Only if we have whipped cream," said Lily, purposely being annoying.

Michael checked the refrigerator door for the squirt kind and there was a new can, which he held up for Lily's approval. Her annoyance level fell a little bit. Michael opened the pudding mix carton and dumped it into a pot. Lily measured out two cups of whole milk while Michael stirred with a whisk. There was no piece of equipment Michael didn't love, including kitchen equipment. She could see him owning a hardware store someday, or a sports store. It would fail, though, because Michael was so silent he'd never sell anything.

Her heart was gripped again by her grief for Michael, who was not the person he was supposed to be. What kind of fourth-grade boy comforted his sister and made her chocolate pudding? He should be off with Jamie, being noisy and hard to find and up to no good.

If only Nathaniel for once in his life could be hard to find. Instead, he was out of Kells's lap and yanking on their elbows, demanding to stir, and wanting to be the one to pour it into dessert cups.

"Like we'd let you pour chocolate pudding," said Lily. "The floor would have more to eat than we would."

"We could have a whipped cream fight," suggested Michael.

"No!" yelled Kells from the recliner.

The front door opened, the screen door slammed, car doors were opened and more doors slammed, as if dozens of people were coming home, but it was only Mom and Rebecca, laden with purchases, flushed with success. The department store and specialty shop bags, with their bright colors and twine handles, meant that they had gone without her to the best malls. "There was school today," Lily said to her mother, the teacher.

"I took a personal day. Rebbie and I went everywhere. We got a few little things but nothing major. We simply could not find a wedding gown. That bridal mall? Nothing at all."

"Well, actually, hundreds of gowns," Rebecca corrected. "But nothing perfect. My wedding is going to be perfect."

"We stopped at Antonio's Deli on the way home," said Mom. "I have veal marsala, chicken tetrazzini and four-cheese lasagna." She popped three trays into the microwave, upended a container of Antonio's walnut, cranberry, feta and romaine salad into a bowl, flipped a long thin garlic loaf under the broiler, took a spoonful of Lily's pudding and said, "But we do have colors picked out. White and three shades of pink: deep, deeper, deepest."

Lily was so relieved to be back in the wedding she didn't even complain about the pink end of the spectrum. "What kind of shoes?" she said. Rebecca loved shoes.

* * *

Michael set his chocolate pudding down untouched. Look at all that stuff Mom and Rebecca bought. You knew girls were serious about stuff when they got shoes to match.

Michael tried to tamp down his excitement. Mom and Lily might turn on him if they felt it. Last year when he said he was going to live with Dad, Mom almost went crazy. Nothing must jeopardize the chance to see Dad again.

He washed Nathaniel's hands while Lily set out forks and Rebecca checked to see if the butter had melted on the garlic bread. They carried everything to the back deck so they could eat in the fresh air. Michael always loved the strange trek of carrying everything from a perfectly good table in the kitchen to a less good table outside, the domestic effort his mother would not make for anything else: a picnic.

Lily always had good stories from the orthodontists' office. Michael meant to sit quietly while Lily talked and then casually wedge in a few questions about Dad. But Lily said nothing and Michael could not wait. "Exactly how long till the wedding, Rebecca?" he asked, meaning Exactly how long till Dad gets here?

"Six weeks," she told him. "October twenty-fourth. I'll be busy every second. I have to admit that I thought this would be easier. I'm still surprised the bridal mall was so unhelpful. If everything's that hard, like finding the right reception hall . . ."

His classroom did not have October's calendar up yet. As

soon as it went up, Michael would make a copy and bring it home and cross out the days the way he had last summer when Dad was coming.

Michael did not want to think about the visit he had un-memorized. It was like turning a sock inside out. All sweat and lint. Or maybe stronger than that. More like unlocking a bank vault. And now something as lovely and shining as his sister's wedding was opening the vault. Michael didn't really want to see in. He tried to see around instead. There was, for example, reading. He was kind of good at it now. Dad wouldn't be so ashamed.

Maybe there would be a printed program for the wedding the way there was for everything else in church, and Michael could read out loud for Dad. He would practice ahead of time.

Michael felt blurry, filled with a kind of anxiety and a kind of love that made him want to go out in the driveway and practice layups or something. What had Reb meant, exactly, that Dad would walk her down the aisle? She couldn't walk by herself? What would Michael's role be? How much would he see of Dad?

Vaguely he heard Rebecca accuse Lily of having a temper tantrum. Vaguely he heard Lily say that Rebecca was a brat. He didn't want to be part of any argument. He wanted to luxuriate in the new calendar shape: the six weeks. On the classroom calendar, the thirty days of September were divided into rows across and rows down and you learned to think of them that way. He tried to envision the thirtieth day of September on the classroom calendar and then mentally tack on October, so that its days too formed rows across and down.

Suddenly his mother's voice was very loud. Mom was furious—apparently at *him*.

"What is this?" she demanded. "I've had it! What is going on here anyway? Michael, you begin. What really happened during that visit to your father? How did it involve Lily?"

A sort of cavity developed in his chest. His heart and lungs and rib cage were getting sucked down, and he was out of air. He had one of those dark moments when he was alone, when the car drove away, when there were only strangers, when the phone calls wouldn't go through and he was a thief. "It didn't involve Lily, Mom."

"But what *was* it?"

"It wasn't anything."

"Honestly, Lily," said Rebecca. "In that case, it's time to face what you've done to this family. We'll work through it. I forgive you, Lily. But when Dad—"

"I didn't do a thing to this family!" shrieked Lily. "*He* did it. And don't you start forgiving me, Rebecca Rosetti! I'm the one who's *right*! I've *always* been right!"

Rebecca stood up fast, jarring her glass of water. Kells made a quick save. Naturally Rebecca ignored this. "You made Dad into an *ogre*, Lily, and then you *poisoned* Michael against him. You did it on *purpose*. You haven't let Michael have anything to do with Dad all this time. And as for you, Mother, you are equally responsible. It's *comfortable* for you to have no contact with your ex-husband. You probably *like* Lily's behavior!"

Nathaniel started to whimper.

Michael steadied himself. Both his sisters were piercing him with their eyes. He was expected to be somebody's ally. They were going to slug it out and the result would be that Dad might not come.

"Michael, have you forgotten how to talk?" yelled Rebecca.

No sentence came to mind that would rescue him from failing Dad yet again.

And then Lily began to tell. "Dad wasn't nice to Michael," she said, in the kind of voice that's just getting started, the kind of voice with lots more to say.

"Everybody's not nice some of the time, Lily," said Rebecca. "It's been a whole year. Doesn't Dad deserve another chance? And even if he doesn't deserve another chance, it's only for a weekend. You can smile for forty-eight hours."

"It isn't that simple," said Lily.

"What's the hard part?" said Rebecca, sounding pretty hard herself.

"I can't hug him or pose in pictures with him," said Lily. "I can't introduce him or listen to his voice. I can't look at Kells, who pays for everything, and then smile at Dad, who got *off*. I can't—"

"I don't know why you have to bring money into it," snapped Rebecca. "Money isn't everything. You're so pathetic, Lily, judging a person by money."

"Actually," said Kells, "this *is* partly about money, Rebecca. Weddings are expensive. I'm paying for this, I take it?"

"Fine!" shouted Rebecca. "I'll get married at Freddie's. *His* family isn't obsessed with money."

Nathaniel began to cry.

Rebecca glared at him. Even Lily glared at him. He cried harder.

"Kells," said Mom stiffly, "kindly allow me to handle this." Without another word, their stepfather collected Nathaniel and went back inside the house.

Michael and his sisters and their mother sat alone around the picnic table. Everything in Michael was churning now: memory, mind, guts. He was afraid he would throw up.

Rebecca sighed. "Come on, Michael," she coaxed gently. "It's just us now. You don't have to pretend in front of Kells or set an example for Nathaniel. What's the story? What did Lily do?"

Michael had to end this. He opened his eyes wide, the way Nathaniel did, so he would look as innocent as a tot. "Nothing happened, Rebecca. I missed everybody here so much that I decided to come home. Lily made a big deal of it. But that's okay. I forgive Lily, too."

* * *

No wonder teenagers ran away from home.

Lily stormed away from the picnic table and stomped inside the house. She ran through the kitchen, down the hall, out the front door and down the front steps and turned left on the sidewalk where hedges blocked the view and no one in her backyard could see her. She began to run.

She had no destination in mind. She was running away, not toward.

She still had on the heavy white sneakers she wore only at work so they would stay clean and unscuffed. Still had on the slate blue tie-on scrub pants and the smock-top with the smiley teeth. Maybe if she ran fast enough, the stupid clothes would be a blur and nobody would notice how ridiculous she looked.

She did not consider going to Amanda's, even though it was only a few blocks away. Amanda liked Michael. Amanda would find excuses for him. He didn't have an excuse. He was a rotten, worthless, ungrateful, hateful, lying little creep.

Lily didn't stop running until the stitch in her side was so painful she had to walk. But slowing down didn't mean turning around. "Jesus!" she said, and she knew she was a lot closer to swearing than praying.

She let herself say it again, and in the same way. She had always wondered why everybody—Christians and non-Christians, atheists and believers—swore using Jesus' name. Now she knew. It worked. His name was real, and swearing by it was really and truly swearing.

A thunderstorm was threatening. The sky got greasy and the air was stifling. She was dripping with sweat. A damp clump of hair crept down her neck.

When she had covered a couple of miles, she found herself at a middle school on whose soggy field she'd played a lot of soccer. Thunder was booming softly in the distance. Threads of lightning split the sky.

Out in the middle of the playing field, Lily Rosetti yelled at God. No roof and no steeple got in her way; no format, no ritual.

"There is no friend at midnight, God! All that stuff about 'seek and you will find'! Being abandoned is what life is all about. *Everybody* abandons you, even the ones you went and saved!"

The storm rolled closer but the rain didn't come. The sky just thickened, like her heart. She knew perfectly well that an open field in a lightning storm was a dangerous place. "*Families* are a dangerous place," she muttered. She walked slowly off the grass, daring lightning to strike her.

She circled school buildings, coming out on a wide four-lane road more residential than commercial, and ran again until sweat was coursing down her body and the stitch in her side was torment.

Half of her wanted to grab the next bus into New York City, live in a gutter and show her family a thing or two.

The other half of her wanted a nice hot shower and clean hair. She tried to laugh but couldn't.

I'll be okay if I can laugh, she said to herself. Jesus, she prayed, let me laugh. Somehow let me laugh instead of rage.

A car pulled up beside her. The driver rolled down all his windows. "Lily?"

"Trey? What are you doing here?"

"I sort of followed you. I went over to Amanda's house to ask her what was going on with you and she told me and then I drove over to your house just as you were slamming your front door. The house practically collapsed. I figured you weren't just going out for fresh air. I've sort of been driving behind you."

So Amanda had also betrayed her, telling Trey the family secrets that Amanda absolutely knew were nobody else's business. But Lily was too tired to stand now, never mind run, so she got in the car with Trey.

They drove around pointlessly until Trey sighted some golden arches. "Two cheeseburgers, two small fries, two vanilla shakes," he said at the drive-in. There was nobody ahead of them. The order was ready in a minute. Trey pulled into a diagonal slot and divided up the food.

She left her cheeseburger in its wrapper. She despised cheese. She hadn't asked for it and she wasn't under any obligation to eat it. He should have asked her first. Everybody in her whole life should have asked her first.

"Hot and salty," said Trey, downing his burger in two bites. "Never fails me. Although April and Ashley have become vegetarians and claim to be comforted by celery."

April and Ashley were each other's best friends, tiresome in the way of twins, with little time for others. They were excellent students and fine athletes and had great hair.

The thunderstorm faded away into the north. Lily sat

silently in the dark car while Trey ate her cheeseburger and fries too. She hung on to the milk shake, sipping it slowly. She wanted a vanilla life, cool and smooth and easy. How did you do that? Amanda had it. How awful to be trapped in this car with this person who knew her too well, and yet knew nothing of how terrible one person could be to another. Who had probably never even *met* a terrible person, let alone had one for a father. And now, as it turned out, Lily had a terrible person for a brother, too.

"What happened that time you were in Anger Management anyway?" asked Trey.

"I got mad at Kells. He was eating popcorn from this big pottery bowl and saying stupid things, so I grabbed the bowl and threw it through the television screen."

Trey laughed. "Sweet."

"They said I wasn't dealing properly with my emotions. But I *am* dealing properly with my emotions. My family are the ones with the emotional problems. Previously I hated just one person in my family. Now I hate them all."

She and Trey burst into convulsive laughter, the kind she generally shared only with Amanda. "I don't want to talk to you about it," she told him. "I hate anybody with a perfect family. Like you."

"What am I supposed to do about that? Beat up on Ashley and April? Vandalize schools? Anyway, you do so have a perfect family. You've got terrific little brothers and a terrific older sister and a nice sunny life in a nice sunny house, and a stepfather who never lets Michael down and a terrific mother. You've got a best girlfriend and you do well in school and you make friends easily. So what is there to whine about?"

"I am not *whining*, I am *right*. They want me to forgive Dad. Well, I won't. Not ever."

"Okay, so hold off on the forgiveness. Take it one commandment at a time."

"What one commandment are you thinking of? I haven't followed any lately."

"You took care of your brother. Jesus is into that."

She squeezed the paper cup that had held her milk shake, and when she'd made a rope of it, she twisted the rope into a cable.

"Remind me never to let you get your hands around my throat," said Trey.

* * *

Michael knew better than to let the topic of Lily continue. He ran inside the house and yelled, "Kells! Nathaniel! Dessert!" After coffee, ice cream, chocolate pudding and cookies, they were all quite civil, and then Nathaniel begged to play badminton in the dark.

Kells put up the net, Nathaniel distributed the rackets and they divided up, boys against girls. In the softening dusk, the feathery white birdies whiffled around like tiny slow comets.

Michael helped Nathaniel when it was his turn to serve. Reb screamed the way a good big sister should—"Oh, no! I'll never get that, Nate! It's too high!"—and then she hit it good and slammed it back, planning to win, but Kells flipped it as neatly as a hamburger back over the net, and it made a soft birdlike whump on the grass.

It seemed to Michael that he might be stuck forever in this half-light, leading a half-life, thinking half-thoughts.

Michael was not old enough to pray. He didn't know how, he couldn't get at it. Formless desperation filled him instead. Lily had saved him and this was how he repaid her.

He felt himself sliding down into a pit of silence, where he could never talk to anybody about anything, because the wrong words would come out, or the wrong actions, or the wrong test results.

Michael served hard and his birdie soared past Mom.

Lily just had to get over it.

Dad had to come.

★ ★ ★

"Where do you want me to drive you, O most irritating person in New York State?" asked Trey.

Lily had no answer and she didn't trust her voice anyway. In the absence of instructions, Trey drove her home.

Churches were extended families, and like families, the people in the pew with you could be so exhausting. She had known Trey forever. Since seventh grade, they'd been in Youth Group together, meeting every Sunday afternoon for activities and prayer. Everybody liked activities and nobody liked prayer. Prayer was embarrassing. Only Amanda was never embarrassed by prayer, and the other kids held her in awe, because her friendship with God was like her friendship with anybody else. She was always yelling at God, giving God orders, confiding in God, chatting with Him as if they were at a slumber party together, and delivering to God her poor opinion of His failure to act again this week.

Amanda's belief was entire; it was that thing called faith. Maybe Lily wasn't getting anywhere because there were so many holes in her belief. Maybe you only got hope and help if you were complete to start with.

"In my opinion," said Trey, when he had pulled up in

front of Lily's house, "not that you asked for it or anything, but you did drink the milk shake I paid for . . ."

"Fine. Whatever. Give me your opinion."

"You're not up to seventy times seven yet."

Lily got out of his car. She forced herself to say thank you for the ride and the shake. She did not thank him for his advice.

She could tell from the laughter and the whiffling floppy sounds that the rest of her family was out in the backyard playing badminton in the dark. She realized suddenly that none of them knew she'd ever been gone. Probably figured she was upstairs sulking in her room.

"How come you're never on my side, Jesus?" she said to Him. "I'm the one who's right."

Does that matter? asked a still small voice.

Lily had considered Michael a jerk for wanting to please Dad, which was like wanting to please God. You're never going to hear from him, so why bother?

Lily had just heard from Him.

*
chapter

14

Saturday morning Lily opened her eyes just long enough to see that the sky was blue and the sun yellow. Turning her face toward the soft breeze coming in her open window, she snuggled herself back in the direction of more sleep.

"Lily!" yelled Rebecca, flinging open the bedroom door. Rebecca dive-bombed Lily's bed, years of practice giving her the skill to bounce Lily half off the mattress but just miss cracking skulls. "It's practically lunchtime, Lily. Hope you weren't planning on straightening any teeth this morning."

"Oh no!" shrieked Lily, leaping out of bed, thrashing around the room, plunging into things and finally coming up with her calendar. "Whew! I don't work today."

Rebecca was laughing. "I knew that. I called your office to make sure I didn't have to wake you up. It was like old home week, talking to all my old orthodontists and assuring them that I still wear my retainer."

"*You do?*" said Lily, very impressed. Nobody bothered with that in real life.

"Of course not. But that's what you say to your orthodontist, isn't it? Listen, Freddie's here. We're back from our wedding conference. Get dressed, I want you to meet him. Wear pink. We'll match."

Their eyes met, declaring a silent truce.

Rebecca blew Lily a kiss and dashed out of the room and down the stairs.

Lily slid over to her open window and looked through the folds of the curtain. Right below her, the man who had to be Freddie was shaking hands with Nathaniel.

Nathaniel said, "Guess what, Feddie. I have a really good Band-Aid."

Freddie admired the Band-Aid, which Nathaniel peeled back to show off his wound. "Wow," said Freddie. "Did you run into fifty guys with swords?"

Nathaniel giggled. "It's a paper cut. You know what? I haven't learned to read yet. Michael says reading is torture."

"No, no. You'll love reading, Nathaniel," said Freddie. "I love reading."

"Oh, please, Freddie, you're an engineer," said Rebecca. "You hardly know the alphabet." Freddie and Rebecca kissed each other above Nathaniel's head. Nathaniel did not care for this waste of time. "Let's play kokay!" he shouted. "Daddy got me a kokay set, Feddie. It's yellow and blue and red and green." Nathaniel offered a huge incentive. "You," he said kindly, "can be red."

"Awesome," said Freddie. "I love red. But I've never played croquet. You teach me."

"Okay," said Nathaniel, handing out mallets. He smiled up at his future brother-in-law and did an amazing thing, something he had refused to change no matter how Lily coaxed and bribed. He pronounced his *l*'s right. "Let's play," he said. And then, visibly working hard, he added, "Frrreddie."

The power of a brother. How huge it was. Even a three-year-old knew; even about a brother who wasn't a brother yet. You did your best for them. You tried to impress them.

She looked around for Michael but couldn't see him from her narrow view. She studied her sister's pink, which was very pale this time, and since Lily personally was not featuring any pink in her closet suitable for the weather, she decided white would match, and after she had white shorts and a white shirt, she invaded Rebecca's suitcases to get a pink scarf and a pink belt. She briefly considered the hideous pink ankle socks Rebecca had in there, but there was such a thing as going too far.

Then she ran downstairs. She paused in the kitchen doorway. Mom and Kells were having coffee at the picnic table on the deck. Michael was still not visible. Freddie was as handsome as his photos. Tall and tan in khaki shorts with many pockets and a khaki shirt with many pockets and a belt with many loops, Freddie was equipped for mountain climbs. He had the half-shaved look of a man who has just climbed a difficult peak.

Lily figured that meeting your in-laws for the first time qualified as a difficult peak.

She went outside laughing at this thought, and Freddie Crumb turned at the sound of her step, and grinned, and opened his arms. "My new sister!" greeted Freddie, giving her a brotherly hug. "Am I glad to meet you at last, Lily. Of course, I've read every one of your e-mails to Reb, so I know all about school this year, and Amanda, and Drs. Bence, Alzina and Gladwin. I especially love when you take the Afters and tell us how everybody makes a perfect After."

"Let's play!" said Nathaniel impatiently.

Freddie lifted his mallet thoughtfully. "How many of us can play croquet at one time? Freddie, Rebecca, Nathaniel, Michael and Lily. Are there enough mallets for five or do we share? Michael, how about you and I share? Red is a big enough color for two."

Lily loved him.

Reb had made a good choice. It wasn't a good choice to drop out of college, but Freddie—he was a seriously good choice.

Freddie extended the handle of his red mallet and Michael stepped forward. He'd been in the shadow and shelter of the high part of the deck, where the flower boxes were built in. She had a ghastly image of Michael seeking shadow instead of sun, stepping back instead of forward, waiting his turn instead of racing to the finish line.

Quicker than her next breath, she thought, Jesus, and He knew, in that strange way of His, what her prayer had to be: Don't let me get angry.

And blessedly, wonderfully, although Lily held her father completely responsible for the changes in Michael, and although she did not soften by one molecule toward denrose, she did not get angry.

"There are plenty of mallets," said Michael. "Mom? Kells? Want to play?"

From the deck, they lowered the newspapers Lily knew they had not been reading. There was a pause, one of those breathless moments neither light nor dark, just very still.

And Rebecca said, "Yes, do! Come on, Kells! Come on, Mom! Let's all play."

Everybody played slowly and incompetently so Nathaniel didn't fall behind.

Every time Nathaniel swung he missed. But Nathaniel never minded. He just kept whacking until he finally connected. Usually he was facing the wrong way. Freddie gave him extra points every time he shot out of bounds and pretty soon, Nathaniel had way the most points. Since croquet didn't even *have* points, nobody had any hope of catching up to Nathaniel.

When Nathaniel hit Freddie's ball out of bounds, Freddie clutched his heart and fell onto the grass, crying, "I'm dead, you killed me!"—nothing could make a three-year-old happier. Nathaniel jumped on Freddie's chest.

"Ow," said Freddie, for real.

"It doesn't hurt," said Nathaniel impatiently. "You're dead."

They were all laughing.

Wedding laughter. Giddy, frothy, blessed laughter.

* * *

The grill was dragged out. Cole slaw and potato salad were prepared. Hamburgers were dropped over the coals. Rolls were toasted. "I squirt the ketchup," yelled Nathaniel, bringing out green and purple.

Freddie gagged. "Our children, Rebecca, will never be permitted green or purple ketchup."

"A can-do rule," said Rebecca.

"Are you going to have a lot of rules?" asked Nathaniel.

"That's my third rule for Rebecca so far," Freddie told him.

"What are the other two?" Michael wanted to know.

"No tuna fish in the house. I hate the smell. People who want to eat tuna fish have to eat it someplace else and brush their teeth before entering. And no fair reading during a meal. There has to be eye contact and talk."

"I'd never break that rule," said Michael, happy. "Rebecca, what are your three rules for Freddie?"

"*He's* allowed three rules for *me*," said Rebecca, "but I've reserved six hundred and fifty rules for *him*."

"That's a lot of rules," said Nathaniel anxiously.

"Yeah, I'm worried," said Freddie, with a huge grin that said he never worried, especially not about Rebecca Rosetti.

Mom said softly to Lily, "Help me in the kitchen, honey?"

It was code. It had nothing to do with kitchens or help. Lily followed her mother inside. She turned just before going in the door to look back at the others, and she saw them as if captured in a photograph: Michael happy, Nathaniel squirting, Freddie teasing, Rebecca in love, Kells in the background.

Mom shut the kitchen door gently behind her. "I'm feeling marginally better about Reb getting married so soon," she said in an undertone. "Actually, I'm not feeling better, but I'm pretending I feel better. I remember when your father left."

Even when Lily hated Dad, she didn't want to hear anything about the divorce. And right now, she desperately didn't want to hear about divorce. She wanted to think of true love and new brothers.

"He was tired of me," said Mom. "Tired of the house, tired of making sure the oil got changed and the lawn got mowed and the doctors' appointments got kept and the new shoes bought. He got tired of my music and tired of—" She broke off. "And when I met Kells, Kells was like a teddy bear.

Plump and soft and kind. Reliable and decent and pre-dictable. And he has been, Lily. I'm so pleased that Reb was nice to Kells. Kells probably will have to pay for the wedding. He earns twice what I do. I can't imagine Dennis suddenly writing checks to a caterer and a florist."

"Try not to worry about it, Mom. Rebecca is going to live on the Arctic Circle, so whether or not she gets along with Kells—"

"I have to cope with your father, though!" When Mom referred to Dennis, she never spoke of him as her ex-husband, but always as "your father." Lily found it pretty tiresome to be Dennis's owner.

"Dennis will be here for two days, maybe three, maybe a *week*, for the wedding," said Mom. "I can't avoid him. I'll have to endure his contemptuous looks at Kells. He'll shudder at this messy house just the way he used to shudder, even though he never once picked up a single thing himself, or ran a vacuum, or sorted mail. It makes my heart pound just to think of keeping my nerves in order with Dennis around. Not to mention pulling off a wedding in six weeks. Lily, I'm a wreck."

Mom doesn't even know I'm suffering, thought Lily. She's not going to comfort me. She thinks *she* needs the comforting. *Comfort ye, my people, saith the Lord.* "Get him a motel room," said Lily.

Her mother gave a desperate little smile at the wall. "Darling, now don't get mad. Take this in the spirit in which it is meant. Rebbie told Dr. Bordon how you don't want to be in the wedding because of your attitude toward your father. Dr. Bordon wants a chat with you this afternoon. In his office. At church."

Lily was so mad she left the house then and there before

she told everybody what she really thought of them. She'd walk to church, but first she might as well stop at Amanda's to whine for a while.

You know what annoys me about you, Jesus? she said to Him. It's having to ask you all the time. You know perfectly well I need you throughout the day and I shouldn't have to repeat myself. You should just be here, making things easier. And now I have to listen to your minister mouth off.

Dr. Bordon was going to look at her compassionately. Lily hated compassion. It was just another word for pity. Like—My life is good and yours isn't, so I'll sit here and bestow my loving glances upon you and get credit for a good deed.

At Amanda's, no time seemed to have passed; no position had changed; no event had taken place. Amanda was still lying under the sun near the pool, ready to listen. When Lily finished the latest episode, Amanda said, "What's up with Michael anyway? And for that matter, what's up with you?"

"I don't know anymore. Don't interrogate me."

"Tell Dr. Bordon what's going on. He's bound to have ideas."

"No. I have enough people pushing me around."

"He's not so bad."

"He'll side with them! He'll tell me to try harder and be nicer and shoulder responsibility." Lily began hurling rubber duckies one by one into the pool. She tried to hit the first ducky with the next ducky. The duckies just bobbed happily, not knowing they were weapons and victims and they were supposed to cry in pain and get hurt and sink.

Amanda was giggling.

Lily was not. "Amanda, I don't want Michael forgiving Dad!"

"You lose," said Amanda. "He already has."

* * *

The church had its Saturday feel—the busy open-door feel of when the sanctuary was just a side room, and the real action was in the community rooms.

Volunteers were loading the soup kitchen donations and collating the bulletins for tomorrow's church service. Parents were getting ready for the middle school sleepover, the ROMEOs (Rowdy Old Men Eating Out) were just getting back from lunch, the Christmas Bazaar committee was finishing its first meeting of the season, and the volleyball team was drifting in for afternoon practice. In the background was the growl of the vacuum cleaning up the church, while the organist hacked away at a pedal part he didn't seem to be conquering. The Sunday school superintendent was arranging piles of new curricula; the weekend class of Bible 101 was arguing in the hallway while the local chapter of Alcoholics Anonymous smoked their cigarettes out in the parking lot.

Church had three parts. The Sunday-morning service/Sunday school part. The Bible class/soup kitchen part. The maintenance part—vacuuming, practicing, repairing the steeple clock. Now Lily saw there was a fourth part. The part where the church interfered.

She imagined Dennis conning everyone, certainly including Dr. Bordon, who knew nothing. Dennis had even conned his victim, Michael, who had forgiven before Lily even got on the plane to rescue him. In fact, since Michael had never held anything against Dennis, there had been no need for forgiveness.

She knocked on the minister's office door.

All four women collating programs turned to see who was seeking help. It was rare for a teenager to consult the minister of her own free will. Possibly something really terrible was going on, in which case, who did they know, so they could phone and get details?

It came to Lily that the person she could never forgive was Michael.

He had thrown in her face all the effort and love she had given him. He had lied about the most important and dangerous thing she had ever undertaken and the biggest achievement she had ever accomplished. Denrose she still despised and denrose she would not smile at or be in a wedding picture with—but Michael was worse.

He hadn't just lied. He had *betrayed*; that biblical word you never encountered in real life. Michael had betrayed her.

"Hi, Lily, come on in," called Dr. Bordon.

Lily went in. She would treat this the way orthodontist patients treated their visits: Go ahead: poke, pry, tighten, glue, whatever. I'm just holding my breath till it's over.

Dr. Bordon wanted to chat about school and her foreign languages and Youth Group but Lily didn't want to, and he was forced to give up. He launched into his sermonette. "When a woman plans her wedding, Lily, she's also planning her future family. She'll have a new family—her in-laws. And she'll add to her family—her future children. A wedding is worth every minute of planning and preparation because it's a holy day in which the family of the bride and the family of the groom rejoice together. So a wedding is about family. Your sister needs you to tolerate the presence of one man in your family for one day."

Rebecca had not needed her family since the day she'd left for college. She had not needed Lily since that moment when she had purposely packed too much so that a half brother and a younger sister couldn't fit in the car.

"Divorce creates pain," said the minister. "The rift can be

impossible to bridge. Nobody is asking you to bridge it, Lily. But—"

Lily snapped. "They are *so* asking me to bridge it."

"You have only one sister, you have only one father. I have no doubt it will be painful for you to do this. But it will be a great gift to your sister."

Who never gave me anything, thought Lily. Not like I gave Michael.

"Lily, I'm one of the many people who drove by the day that Michael sat on the curb, waiting ten hours for his father to show up. I'm one of the ones who called to see what I could do. I'm one of the ones who wasn't surprised when Michael's hopes for his father didn't work out. I'm one of the ones who trembled for Michael, and when he was back home, I prayed that he'd come out of his frozen state and be as laughter-filled as when he left."

Lily spoke fiercely. "I don't see why we bother with a God you have to pray to and pray to. Once should be enough. He should be listening the first time."

"I often feel that way. But we're caught in the web of what other people decide to do. We can't escape the results of other people."

"I was escaping just fine," said Lily. "And Rebecca is wrecking things."

"No matter how you've been hurt," began Dr. Bordon—but Lily couldn't stand it anymore.

"You know nothing!" she yelled. "You're a beginner in the world of hurt. You're junior varsity. I'm a pro."

Dr. Bordon looked at her for some time.

All of a sudden she knew that he was thinking the same thing Trey's father had thought about what Dennis had done to Michael. "You watch too much television," she accused him, although he was at the church practically every night of the week teaching or participating or leading and she knew perfectly well he never had time for television. "I can tell you're thinking he did something sexual to Michael. Well, he didn't. He was just scum. He's always been scum, he's still scum, he'll always *be* scum, and I won't be in a wedding with him!"

Dr. Bordon nodded for a while. "Just give it some thought," he said finally, "and some prayer."

"What do you think I've been doing? Giving it potato chips?"

Dr. Bordon laughed. "One time in the Youth Group I decided to serve a snack Communion, so we had Coke and potato chips instead of grape juice and bread. But kids are always serious, even when they say they hate being serious. Nobody would take a potato chip. The toughest kid there, who showed up just to pick on everybody else, explained to me that Jesus was not about potato chips." He was still laughing when he added, "Jesus," before Lily spotted the prayer coming, "be with Lily."

* * *

Mom, Kells, Rebecca, Freddie and Michael were sitting in the shade of the blue and green striped awning on the deck, talking companionably. Every one of them looked up at the intruder who was Lily.

Right away she knew she was going to pick a fight.

"*Crumb?*" Michael was saying. "My sister's new last name will be *Crumb*?"

Michael was teasing Freddie. It had been exactly a year since the last time Michael had been able to tease.

"I think you should have planned ahead, Reb," said Michael, "and fallen for a guy with a great last name."

"Excuse me," said Freddie. "The Crumbs have a long, impressive background."

"Of what?" said Michael. "Sandwiches?"

"Michael, you're not going to be able to say anything about my last name I haven't already heard. I made sure Rebecca was hopelessly in love with me before I said my last name out loud. And if she wants to stay Rebecca Rosetti, I'll understand."

"You could be Freddie Rosetti."

"Nope. I'm stronger, tougher, and more interesting because I've had to survive being a Crumb."

"But your kids have to be little Crumbs."

"Yup. And I'll be proud when they lift their heads high and admit to being Crumbs," said Freddie.

Out in the yard, Nathaniel was still playing croquet. There were no balls visible. He had probably hit them all into the bushes. He was now prying up croquet wickets and wearing them as a necklace. Lily decided he couldn't strangle himself, since they had large openings, so she didn't get involved.

Rebecca came bounding over. "Did you have a nice talk with Dr. Bordon?" she asked, brightly as a nursery school teacher.

"Couldn't talk it over with me yourself?" asked Lily. "Had to ask a minister to handle it for you?"

"It isn't possible to talk to you. You won't listen. I thought you might listen to Dr. Bordon," said Rebecca stiffly.

Lily would have run away from home, but she hadn't rested up from running away the last time. She went into the kitchen, opened the freezer, got out an ice cream sandwich, took off the wrapper and licked a vanilla path around the chocolate wafers. Then she went out to the deck.

Freddie patted the picnic table to invite her over. Lily sat across from him. It wasn't a great position because she was also facing Rebecca. "So everything's fine?" said Freddie. "You're going to be the maid of honor?"

"We're still having trouble on the father front," Rebecca said.

Freddie leaned forward. He looked very earnest. "I know it's tricky to deal with your dad," said Freddie, as if he could possibly know. "You guys haven't seen him or talked to him in a year."

Michael said, "But you have, Freddie." Michael's eyes were wide and unblinking, but he wasn't looking at anybody. "How is he?"

"Seems like a great guy," said Freddie. "But then, we didn't get into the hard stuff, like how he's never paid child support."

Michael was stunned. His face took on a sick yellow color.

Lily watched Michael try, and fail, to sip some of his soda.

Nobody else seemed to be looking at Michael. They were all looking at her. *She* was the bad guy here.

"When we went camping together, I liked the guy, Lily," said Freddie, as if it were any of his business; as if he had any right to pitch a tent with denrose, who couldn't even be bothered to acknowledge he had two other kids!

If I start screaming, thought Lily, I'll be the person who is behaving the worst, when in fact, I'm the person who's behaving the best.

"Dr. Bordon and Freddie and I had such a good good good talk this morning," said Rebecca. "Dr. Bordon says one beautiful thing about a wedding is how it brings families together. A wedding is an occasion for rejoicing. To make the rejoicing complete, every member of the family must be present."

Lily folded her hands in her lap. Then she knotted them into fists. She cut her palms with her own fingernails.

"What did Dr. Bordon suggest we should do about your difficulties, Lily?" asked Rebecca. "I mean, we're all ready to pitch in here."

"I think it's Lily's affair what she and her minister discussed," said Kells mildly.

"They discussed *my* wedding," said Rebecca, "and that makes it *my* business, Kells. If you would like to butt out of this discussion, feel free."

Kells withdrew, as he always did. He had stated his position, but he didn't argue. Lily didn't know if she envied him or despised him.

"I just hope you're ready to call Dad and be perfectly, utterly pleasant," said Rebecca to her sister.

"With a nail gun in my hand," said Lily.

She knew Freddie was appalled.

She knew Mom was embarrassed.

She knew Michael was frozen in place, wanting nothing to touch his vision of Dad coming.

She and her sister went at it as they had not done in years. Even in middle school, when Lily would torment Rebecca constantly, they had never done anything like this, because each sister could escape into her own room. They yelled long enough for Freddie to try to separate them; long enough for Mom to cry, "Girls!"

Lily did not know how long they had been yelling when Kells rejoined them. Rebecca was midsentence. Kells interrupted. Rebecca glared. If there was one thing she could not stand, it was a stepfather, and if there was one thing worse, it was a stepfather who dared to talk when she had the floor.

"Where's Nathaniel?" said Kells.

chapter
15

He was three.

Their yard was not fenced.

And they had no idea how long he had been gone.

They looked in the bushes and under the deck. They looked in the garage and in the cars, in the toolshed and in the cellar. They looked in the bedrooms and under the beds. They looked down the sidewalks and on the neighbors' porches.

I did this, thought Lily. I know how Nathaniel hates raised voices. I raised my voice meaner and harsher and angrier than I ever have. I did it because I felt like it, not because I had to. It was me he ran from.

Her knees were trembling.

Nathaniel, who was not afraid of cars, intersections or strangers. Nathaniel, who had never gone through a No stage. Who would say yes to anybody about anything.

I did this, thought Rebecca. I saw him put those stupid wire hoops around his neck and I thought, Good grief, the kid could strangle himself, and I didn't do anything because he's from a marriage I wish hadn't happened. I could have gone out in the yard and picked him up and put away the croquet set and he'd be here at the table right now.

I don't want Mom happy with her second husband. So I just sat here and thought—the kid's their problem. So there.

But every little kid is always your own problem.

I did this, thought Michael. I've been lying and Nathaniel always knew. He tried so hard to tell about his airplane ride but over and over I let Kells say, No, only Michael went on a plane—as if Nate's too dumb to know the difference. Lily rescued me and Nathaniel rescued me just as much, and I lied about them.

I knew Nate was walking farther and farther away from us because he didn't like the screaming. But I couldn't interrupt the screaming because Lily would notice me and then she'd yell at *me* and it would all come out.

I wanted what Dad did to me to be a secret, more than I wanted to bother with my little brother.

They fanned out.

They covered front yards, backyards, around the block one way, around the block the other.

"What friends of his live nearby?" asked Freddie, when they had all collected in the front yard again.

"He's three," said Mom. "He doesn't go anywhere. We take him."

Kells said, "Dial nine-one-one."

"Wait," said Lily. "He might go to Amanda's. He loves the walk. He likes a yard around the corner that has plastic gnomes and pink flamingoes."

"He might go in Amanda's swimming pool," agreed Michael.

"He might be alone at a swimming pool?" cried Kells.

Freddie wore his cell phone on a hook attached to his amazing khaki shorts. Lily ripped it out of his hands and called Amanda.

The dialing of a phone is such a short space of time. The slightest fraction of a minute. Two heartbeats. One deep breath. But in that time, so many prayers can be heard.

Please, God, don't let the pool gate be open.

Please, God, if Nathaniel opens the gate, don't let him go in the pool.

Please, God, if he goes in the pool, let him be okay.

I'll do whatever you want if you just protect Nathaniel.

"Oh, hi," said Amanda. "I was just about to call. Nathaniel's here, all upset from the screaming and yelling, and he wants to live with me and I said of course, forever, I love you, you're perfect and he said, Then can I have ice cream? The thing about three-year-olds is, Lily, they're honest. It all comes down to ice cream. Who dishes it out and who doesn't. I," said Amanda with satisfaction, "am a disher-out."

Kells sagged.

Mom wept on his shoulder.

Reb went limp against Freddie.

"How long has he been there?" Lily asked.

"Who knows? I found him asleep by the pool, wrapped up in my towels with my rubber duckies lined up beside him. He didn't go in the water without me, he's such a good kid."

We're all good kids, thought Lily.

"We'll be there in a minute, Amanda," said Lily. "Mom, Kells, Rebecca, Freddie, Michael and me."

"I get to meet Freddie? Is he as cute as his pictures?"

"Cuter," said Lily, and not only did she love Freddie, she loved Reb again, could even remember that nicknames were for when you felt affection.

Kells ran for his car keys and brought the van around and they piled in, Michael and Freddie in the back, Reb and Lily in the middle, Mom and Kells in front. Kells backed out of the driveway so fast that if any three-year-old *had* been passing by, he'd have been mushed flat.

Michael talked fast and loud to get it over with. It was easier because everybody's back was to him and he didn't have to meet their eyes. "I lied. Nathaniel knew what happened, but he's so little you didn't believe him. He was telling the truth. Here's what happened. Last summer I never wanted to come home. I wanted to be with Dad. But I wasn't good enough for him. He didn't tell me what we were doing. I didn't have anything with me. We just got in the car and he dropped me off at the airport and said, 'You're not the son I had in mind,' and then he drove away. He never even bought me a plane ticket. I didn't have York because Dad threw York in the trash to make me grow up. I didn't have any money either, or my watch, or even breakfast. I called Lily and she bought plane tickets with her Christmas money and she and Nathaniel flew to the Baltimore/Washington airport to get me and when we flew home, I made her promise never ever ever to tell you because—" Michael had to stop. Not because he was crying. Because everybody else was crying. Michael raised his voice. "Because it was not what I thought would happen. I thought Dad and I would play catch."

"Oh, Michael!" cried Mom. "Why didn't you tell me?"

"I love Dad," said Michael simply. "Lily doesn't love Dad, but she loves me." He said to Lily, "I'm sorry."

"Michael," whispered Rebecca, "I didn't know."

Kells was taking the corners very hard. Lily thought it would be totally crummy if they all died in a car accident on the way to get Nathaniel, who was perfectly safe with Amanda. Crummy, she thought. She looked at Freddie.

He put out his hand and covered hers. "I'll be proud to be your brother, Lily."

"I had to hide out in the airport for four hours," Michael said, "because it took Lily that long to come and get me. I didn't want the security people to pick me up, but they almost did. And then I didn't even get to the baggage claim to meet Lily when I was supposed to because I was holding a teddy bear at a store and the police thought I was shoplifting and Nathaniel came and saved me and Lily bought the bear."

Mom was weeping. But it was Reb who got angry. "Wait a minute," said Reb, in her dangerous voice, the one she had inherited from Mom. "Let me get this straight, Michael. Dad put you in the car, without breakfast, without your stuff and without a dollar and without York, and he dropped you off at a major airport and drove away and he had not bought you a ticket or made plans for you to get home or called Mom that you were coming or anything?"

"Right. Good thing Lily was home."

"Give me your phone, Freddie," said Reb. She snatched it away from him before he could give it to her and began stabbing at the tiny number pad. Lily remembered a few phone calls she'd made like that. "How dare he!" said Reb. "How dare Dad behave like that? He's not a father! He has no right to *pretend* he's a father! *I will never use that word for him again!*"

Lily took the phone away from her sister.

Kells pulled into Amanda's driveway, shoved the car into park, vaulted out and ran through the swimming pool gate.

Lily gave the phone back to Freddie. "See, here's the thing," said Lily to the family she loved. "You say terrible things to somebody, and they come true. If you tell him he isn't your father anymore, Reb, then he won't be. You and Michael can still love him, Reb. I don't think I can. I'm not willing to try, anyway."

Her sister's eyes met hers. The look between them was not a truce. It was love.

"I was wrong, Lily," said Reb.

"You were wrong about everything! I want a list. I want to spend at least an hour while you admit all the ways you were wrong."

"I was wrong ten ways to Sunday. But I'm right about this," said her sister, and they put their arms around each other, twisting over the seats and getting their tears mixed when their cheeks touched. "I want you to be my maid of honor, and it will be *my* honor."

After such an exciting day, Nathaniel couldn't stay awake through dinner, but after such an exciting day, Kells couldn't bring himself to put Nathaniel down for bed, so instead, Kells held his sleeping son in his arms while the rest of them ate. They didn't do any yelling, in case it woke Nathaniel up, but they argued and wept and accused and made peace. Various suggestions for killing Dennis were passed around, which Lily found very satisfying, but everybody stopped when they saw how Michael was taking it. During dessert, when people were spooning really good ice cream into their mouths, Kells spoke up.

"It sounds as if everybody, including Michael, thinks Dennis shouldn't be part of the wedding."

"It sounds as if everybody except Michael wants Dennis arrested or else assassinated," said Freddie.

There was a round of applause. Michael put down his spoon. The ice cream didn't taste so good after all.

"In the end," said Kells, "this isn't about punishment. It's about love."

Reb glared. "Oh, brother!"

"Exactly. Lily knew all along that it's Michael who pays if we go after Dennis. So let me speak as a stepfather and a person very fond of everyone at this table."

Reb had the decency to blush.

"After the wedding, Rebecca, why don't you and Freddie take at least a few days and go on a honeymoon? Surely your company will grant you that. Then, since you and Freddie like to camp, and you've gone camping twice with Dennis, let's arrange a camping trip. Rebecca and Freddie and Michael and I will go, and Dennis will come. Michael will get to be with his dad and Freddie will make sure we all have fun. But I'll be in charge. Dennis won't be in trouble with the police, but he'll always be in a certain amount of trouble with me. It was such a wrong thing to do. We can't trust Dennis, Michael, but that doesn't mean you can't love him. I have a cousin who's a heroin addict. I can't trust him, but I love him. And that way, Lily doesn't deal with Dennis at all. Maybe someday she'll want to. But not now."

"I like it," said Freddie.

"I don't!" said Rebecca. "I want to make Dennis admit every single disgusting thing he did. I want him punished. Somebody somewhere has to tell Dennis where to go!"

"This isn't about somebody somewhere," said Kells. "It's about Michael."

Michael looked desperately at Reb. His eyes were huger and sadder than Nathaniel's had ever been.

"Okay. Fine," said Reb irritably. "If Lily can give everything she has, I guess I can give one thing I have. I promise, Michael. We'll all go camping and— Wait a minute! Not say anything? Pretend Dennis is a decent person? For what—two or three days? Kells, are you serious? That's impossible!"

"Lily did it."

Rebecca looked at her sister. "I can't believe this is happening to me. I have to follow my little sister's example."

"Then we can do it?" said Michael. "We can go camping with Dad?"

Lily's heart was torn to pieces all over again. She looked at her mother, who was silently trying to understand all that had happened, all that she had not seen. She looked at her future brother-in-law, engineer that he was, taking out his calendar to find honeymoon and camping dates. But mostly she looked at her sister, who was going to have to handle Dennis in person, in a tent. "We can go camping with Dad," promised Reb. "I'll be nice." She looked at Kells.

In all these years, she had never really wasted time looking straight at Kells. She said, "At the wedding, Kells? Would you walk me down the aisle?"

* * *

"I'm giving a pool party next Saturday night, Lily," said Amanda. "I'm inviting everybody. You first, then all our friends, my parents and your parents. I'm totally in love with Kells. I want to marry a dusty blue recliner kind of guy. Then I'm inviting all the Mahannas, because if you're not in love with Trey yet, you should be. And Dr. Bordon. If I knew their names, I'd invite the guy at the ballpark who didn't make Michael pay for the spilled drinks and the airport people who worried about him."

"A celebrate Michael party?" said Lily. "That's so sweet."

"No, you dope. A friend at midnight party for you."

"Me?" said Lily.

"Of course for you."

"Why me?"

"Because you're the friend at midnight."

Lily stared at her.

"*If you had a friend, would you go to that friend at midnight?*" Amanda said. "*Because he is your friend, he will get up and give you everything you need.* Jesus."

"I never heard you swear before."

"I'm not swearing. I'm calling on Jesus to make a dent in your hard head, Lily. It's Dr. Bordon's favorite text. The whole church is totally sick of it. Don't you ever listen? The friend comes downstairs anyway. Even grumpy. Even over something stupid, like they need a loaf of bread to make sandwiches. And here you are crushed and furious and betrayed by your father, your sister and your brother—and still, you came down the stairs to open the door and give."

I'm the friend at midnight? thought Lily. All this time I was yelling at Jesus to pitch in? And He was making sure that *I* was pitching in?

"And finally," said Amanda, "Trey. He's always adored you, Lily. He sits behind you in church so he can watch you during the sermon. Talk about a guy who forgives seventy times seven! I'm going to shove you both in the pool at the same time, and for once in your life, be nice to the guy. And don't ask Jesus for help. Boyfriends you handle on your own."

And friends, too, thought Lily. Friends at midnight, friends at any hour of the day—for friends, O Lord, we give you thanks.

Caroline B. Cooney is the author of *Diamonds in the Shadow; Hit the Road; Code Orange; The Girl Who Invented Romance; Family Reunion; Goddess of Yesterday* (an ALA Notable Book); *The Ransom of Mercy Carter; Tune In Anytime; Burning Up; The Face on the Milk Carton* (an IRA-CBC Children's Choice Book) and its companions, *Whatever Happened to Janie?* and *The Voice on the Radio* (each of them an ALA Best Book for Young Adults), as well as *What Janie Found; What Child Is This?* (an ALA Best Book for Young Adults); *Driver's Ed* (an ALA Best Book for Young Adults and a *Booklist* Editors' Choice); *Among Friends; Twenty Pageants Later;* and the Time Travel Quartet: *Both Sides of Time, Out of Time, Prisoner of Time,* and *For All Time.* Caroline B. Cooney lives in Westbrook, Connecticut, and New York City.